A Different Way of Being

By
ML Dumars

A Different Way of Being

Copyright © 2023 by ML Dumars

All rights reserved.

Acknowledgements

I owe a special thank you to Laura Flett, Sanderia Smith, Debra Roberson, and the Shreveport Writers Club. I also owe a great thank you to the speculative fiction writers who inspired me. To my fans, keep thinking outside the box, and live with passion.

Cover artwork

"Ether" by Whitney Tates. https://wetpaintarts.com

Table of Contents

CHAPTER ONE

The voluminous space of the cylindrical room was filled with climate-controlled quiet and the muffled sounds of pages turning. Muted silver tables and chairs accommodated engrossed readers bathed in still pools of lighting. Strategically placed workstations offered touch screen monitors for quick reference. A polished chrome staircase wound itself along the inside curve of bare walls on either side of the study hall.

The woman scanned the information scrolling up the small screen of the handheld reader as she slowly climbed the stairs to the next level. Expecting another stair, she stumbled onto the landing instead, dropping her reader. A little boy ran over to help her, handing her the viewer she dropped. He smiled up at her and giggled, the tip of his tongue peeking through the space where two baby teeth had recently fallen out. She couldn't help but smile back; his snaggle-toothed grin was so charming.

"Thank you, little one, for saving my Viewer. That would've been the third one I'd have broken this year."

"My name's Benny. Will you play with me?"

Without waiting for a reply, the little boy took her hand and pulled her toward a low table covered with brightly colored translucent shapes. She sighed for a moment, then tucked the Viewer into a pocket and complied, thinking it would be a quick game. As they began the intricate game of acquisition, she quickly noted how advanced he must be to know such complex stratagem.

While he contemplated his next move, she looked around the room. It was a loft overlooking the large study hall below. The décor, or lack thereof, was the same as the lower level, but slightly miniaturized for a children's area. There were other games and activities, but the ones she recognized were all equally as complex. She had taken the wrong stairway, without thinking. This would cost her valuable research time, but she was enjoying the break from routine.

A dark-haired man sat in one of the small chairs at the front of the spacious room, looking over a viewer similar to hers, only the screen was larger and the images appeared to hover in the air above it, obviously a newer model. He cleared his throat and shifted slightly, uncrossing and recrossing his long legs. He seemed too absorbed in his own affairs to be connected in any way with little Benny, but she couldn't imagine the little boy being here alone.

The man stood abruptly, smoothed out his dark clothing and walked toward a discreetly located desk. There sat a librarian, keying in a lock sequence code on the enclosure for the children's readers. He patiently waited for her to acknowledge him.

The woman pushed unruly brown hair from her face, catching the thick mass into a tail while she continued to close up the area for the day. The overhead lighting had already dimmed, letting the patrons know it was closing time. She straightened the chairs and tables, clearing any small debris that had been left by careless visitors. As she approached their table, Benny made his move and won the game. She smiled down at them.

"I won, Mommy."

"Yes, I see that. Now what do you say?"

Benny beamed and reached to shake his opponent's hand. He looked very serious as he thanked the woman still studying the board for her error. She shook his little hand, and stood up. She had not seen that move at all. But her mistake was obvious now that he had beaten her. She was impressed. She smiled politely to excuse herself, when Benny asked her for her name.

"I am called Nedra Landier. And I have kept your mother from closing long enough, I think. I do apologize for not noticing the time, ma'am."

"No, not all. I have enjoyed watching the two of you play. Benny does not often find so worthy an adversary; he actually had to think this time."

As she spoke, the librarian's amber eyes seemed to glow slightly. An unexplained familiarity washed over Nedra, then quickly dissipated when the man near the desk cleared his throat again. He walked over to them and pointed to the empty hall beyond the chrome railing. He spoke in a firm whisper.

"Excuse me, but the building is closing. We must leave now, Je'Nea."

"Yes, we must be quick. Punctuality is a virtue here."

The librarian took Benny's hand and led them all out of the building. Out on the sidewalk, she turned to speak to Nedra, but Benny interrupted. His small voice was excited.

"I want Nedra to come with us," he demanded, taking his new playmate's hand in his free hand.

"Corben, we must not impose on this woman's time any longer. I am sure she has other things to do."

The man stated this with a stern voice. Feeling a little annoyed, Nedra surprised herself by answering. She did not think, just reacted.

"Actually, I have the evening free."

"Then it's settled. Nedra will walk with us in exchange for dinner, and you, Mr. Orin, won't have to worry about us getting safely home since she is a Security Agent."

Je'Nea smiled sweetly as she excused him from his self-imposed obligation. They watched as he sulked away. When he was out of view, Je'Nea chuckled to herself as she turned to walk away.

"He takes things so seriously, but he means well. I, of course, do not expect you to watch over us. You are free to go. Thank you again for spending time with Benny."

Little Corben glanced back sadly, but obediently walked beside his mother. Nedra watched them leave, bewildered. She hurried to catch up with them, grasping Benny's eager hand reaching for hers again.

"Wait a minute. I have a duty to perform, remember. How did you know I'm a Security Agent, anyway?"

Nedra glanced down quickly to make sure she wasn't still in uniform or wearing any gear. The librarian smiled guiltily. She looked straight ahead and increased her pace.

"I just know; I mean I can just tell. You seem like the type. You don't have to walk us. We will be fine."

"Are you brushing me off? Did I do or say something to offend you?"

Nedra was uncertain. Benny's hand left hers. The empty space grew cold where his warm fingers had been. The woman stopped walking, turned to face her.

"I am very grateful to you for being nice to my son. I am also grateful that you are willing to escort us home. But we don't need anyone to take care of us. That's all."

"Mr. Orin obviously thinks you do. And I suspect he would not like it one bit if he knew an Agent had abandoned her assignment. I could get in a lot of trouble, Miss -?."

Nedra tried to hide her grin. However, the librarian seemed agitated. She was not amused.

"My name is Je'Nea Sincera. I am not your assignment and I am certain that you will not get into any trouble on my account. I was wrong to imply it. I do not care for your company any longer."

The woman moved to walk away. Benny began to cry silently. Nedra was disappointed that her teasing had the wrong effect. She caught the woman's arm to stop her but quickly yanked her hand away. It was hot enough to burn.

"Hey, I was just joking. Really. I don't mind walking with you at all. I just wondered how you knew. I'm sorry I was so rude. Come on, little guy, it's ok. Mommy's just a little upset. You be strong and take care of her, ok?"

She knelt next to the little child. Benny wiped his tears and shook his head yes. He took his mother's hand again. Nedra stood, began to apologize again. She had acted like an ass. Real smooth, upset a citizen and make a little child cry. Some agent she was. She was sure to get demerits if this was reported. Je'Nea held up her hand to stop whatever Nedra was about to say.

"Listen, I should be apologizing to you for this misunderstanding. I just did not want to deal with Mr. Orin today. I should not have used you as an excuse and gotten you involved. I knew you would take the wrong stairs and I should have stopped Benny but I did not. I am sorry."

"What do you mean, you knew I would take the wrong stairs? Since I'm already with you, why don't we continue as planned and you can explain."

Nedra took Benny's hand again and they began to walk. She had a feeling the woman had not meant to say that, but that it was true. How could that be?

They were silent. Nedra would be patient. She observed her surroundings as they moved along. The evening was warm. A faint breeze shook the leaves of the young trees marching along the edge of the street. Everything was clean, tidy. The storefronts were neatly organized, unobtrusive. A sign announced the name and the type of store over each uniform doorway. Nothing was out of place. Everyone minded his or her own business. Safety was certainly not a concern here. Nor was it a concern in most of the city. This was one of the oldest metros on the planet. It was conceived in order and order remained its law.

Nedra's duties as a Security Agent were easy. "Be present, be observant, be courteous." Though it was not part of the motto, being anonymous was also expected. The lightweight helmets the agents wore ensured that. She still remembered the initial awkwardness she experienced while trying to adjust to the visual aids inside the visor. The augmentative listening devices were less disturbing than the constant bombardment of visuals and text occupying the corners of her peripheral view.

She ran a hand through the short crinkly hair curling at the nape of her neck. She thought about letting it grow and lock again. She could keep it trimmed neat under the helmet. No one would even notice, certainly not the citizens; they never looked an Agent in the face anyway. A tug on her arm brought her out of her reverie.

Benny was jumping and swinging between the two women, using their arms as support. He bounced up the walkway to the front door. He smiled that crazy smile at Nedra, then began to shimmy around in a circle singing "Getti, getti, I luv getti!" She cast a puzzled glance at his mother. Je'Nea entered the code for the door. She looked embarrassed.

"We did promise you dinner. Tonight is spaghetti night. Benny's favorite. I hope you do not mind."

"You don't have to feed me. I just wanted to make sure you arrived safely home, like I said I would."

"Please, Benny would love if you stayed for dinner. I would too. Don't worry. It is not real meat. We are also vegetarians."

"I guess you just knew that too. I seem like the type, right? Ok, I'll stay for some of Benny's 'getti'."

Nedra laughed at herself. She patted Benny's hand. He held firm. She followed them up three flights of stairs to their living quarters.

The place was modest but homey. Indirect light gave it a glowing effect. Carefully blended colors shimmered from the artwork on the walls. Nedra peered closer at one near her and saw that they were composed of thermal sensitive panels instead of actual paint. Je'Nea offered her a seat in one of the memory form chairs. Benny disappeared down the hall.

"Did you make those on the walls? They are beautiful," she said when the woman nodded yes. Nedra relaxed into the comfort of the chair. The tension of the day drained right out of her body. She hadn't been that relaxed in months. She closed her eyes and let her head clear, feeling her body heat reflected back to her by the chair.

Je'Nea smiled, enjoying the opportunity to look fully at her visitor. She saw the creases around the young woman's eyes melt away. Dark eyebrows arched over thick curly lashes. Her mouth relaxed, full lips slightly parted. The dark pink lips curled in a smile.

"Are you watching me?"

Nedra opened her eyes to look at her host. Je'Nea blushed. She was caught. She went into the kitchen cubicle to prepare their meal. Nedra followed her. She leaned on the counter and watched the woman rehydrate the pasta and shape the tiny protein nodules into little meatballs.

Nedra observed the woman's hands. Long shapely fingers, nails neatly manicured with no hint of added color. Her skin was smooth and brown, a rich chocolate cream. She moved gracefully, as if everything she touched was delicate and beautiful. She was careful and efficient, no movement wasted. She washed her hands and dried them while looking at Nedra.

"Benny and I did the walls ourselves. It was the first thing we did when we moved here. He did his room all by himself. He'll probably show you one day. He's very proud of it."

Je'Nea handed Nedra the eating utensils to place on the table. She busied herself with gathering everything they would need. When the places were set, she called Benny in to join them. They sat around the little table and held hands while Benny said a short but sincere prayer.

After they had eaten their fill, Benny left to take his bath and read before bed. Je'Nea placed the dirty dishes in the particle sterilizer and switched off the lighting in the cubicle. She joined Nedra in the central area.

"Thank you for a wonderful dinner. I see why Benny sings about your 'getti'; it's so good."

Nedra's compliment was answered with another slight blush and a smile. She liked making this woman smile. She also liked that she couldn't figure her out easily. "Alright, now will you answer my questions? You must admit I have been patient."

Je'Nea shook her head. "I thought you were being so attentive because you were enjoying yourself. Sorry to have kept you waiting."

"Don't get me wrong. I am enjoying myself here. I haven't done very much socializing since I was stationed here. I suppose I've become a dull girl. All work, you know."

"I do not find you dull at all. You do work too much, though."

"Excuse me? We just met, remember? You are assuming too much."

"Do not get upset. Besides, you just met me today; I have known you a little longer."

"Oh, have you? And just what do you think you know about me?"

"Well, I know you often take extra patrol shifts because you prefer to be working than sitting around your compartment. I know you come to the research facility every day after your shift ends. I know you prefer the feel of printed material to the impersonal hardness of the digital readers. I also know you like vintage 20th century Earth music and that you have a beautiful singing voice."

Nedra sat quietly listening to this woman, this stranger, tell her intimate details of her life. She should be suspicious and uneasy but she was completely at ease with this woman. There was something unexpected too; a familiar tingle at the base of her spine, steadily spreading through her body. She was attracted to this woman. She wasn't sure if she liked that or not.

"Relax. I do not work for any covert operation. I have seen you in the facility. You always sit in the same general area, near a window preferably. You like to stare out as you contemplate what you have read. You look like you are praying when you tug your bottom lip, like you are doing now."

Nedra's hands were pressed together with the mid fingers touching her bottom lip. She dropped them to her lap. She burrowed them into her pockets.

"When you have a good day, you sing to yourself. When you have a bad day, you hum. Either way, you always have a song in mind. You are particularly fond of Cole Porter and Ella Fitzgerald. The songs are so pretty I looked them up."

"Ok, stop. How can you possibly know all this? What do you do, spy on me? I don't think I like it either."

"Yes, you do. You are sitting there thinking you should not like it, but you do. It is ok to be flattered. I can only be honest with you. I have watched you. I have extraordinarily sensitive ears; I hear what most people cannot. The first time I heard you sing, I looked over the balcony and saw you sitting below in the study hall. You were sitting just as I described you, your lips barely moving. I even remember the song, "Do It Again" by George Gershwin; I looked it up. That is a very provocative song. I have often wondered what or who could have put you in that frame of mind. I wished it had been me." She blushed again and looked away.

Nedra didn't know what to say to this. It was all pretty impossible. Most people have no idea who any of these old Earth musicians were. And she certainly was not used to women coming on to her so strongly, though this woman did not act like she was flirting, just speaking matter-of-factly. She was getting flustered and began to think of a way to graciously excuse herself, when Je'Nea placed her hand on her shoulder.

"Listen, I did not say those things to make you uncomfortable. I just wanted to be honest. I guess I should temper some of the things I say."

Despite her initial tension, Nedra relaxed again, though her attraction was steadily getting stronger. She

fought an overwhelming desire to kiss this woman.
Calm down, girl.

"No, not at all. You just surprised me is all. Ok,
what about the Agent thing. I'm dying to know how you
knew about that? I never wear my uniform off duty."

"Oh, you patrol this area frequently. I can feel
your presence. Like you are feeling mine now."

"What? Don't be silly. Now you're talking like
an Empath." Nedra laughed. That was a good one.
None of those left anyway.

"Why do you think you feel so comfortable with
me? Would you normally have dinner with someone
you just met? Would you be sitting in the home of a total
stranger? You know me, sort of. You feel it, don't
you?"

As she spoke, Je'Nea's voice became softer,
almost a whisper, and she moved closer. Their lips met
in a tender kiss.

Nedra was drifting in a warm place unknown but
familiar. She heard the faint sound of a child's giggles;
saw shimmering images of a little girl playing with her
mother and father. Then she saw a group of children

21

playing a game. She recognized herself, a small awkward child running toward home base, being caught by the opponent just before she reached it. She could see the caretakers' silhouettes up on the hill. She opened her eyes as she pushed Je'Nea away.

"You did not like it? Did I misunderstand?"

Anger swept over Nedra like a swift storm. Her eyes narrowed. Her nostrils flared.

"What the hell are you doing? You *are* an Empath, aren't you? That's why you know so much. Well, you can't just play with normal people's heads. You'd better watch yourself."

Nedra stormed out the door. Je'Nea crumpled on the nearest seat, resisting the urge to cry. She knew better, but she thought this woman would somehow be different. She wouldn't be as closed-minded as the others, wouldn't let prejudice and unfounded fear blind her. Surely, she would see her as a normal person like everyone else. She was wrong and it hurt more than she could bear. She went to her room and cried herself to sleep.

It had been two weeks since Je'Nea and Benny decided to venture into the confectioner's shop and try something new. Every evening since then, they stopped to see what the flavor magician had come up with that day. There were so many ways to tempt and tantalize the palate. They found they both liked the peppery flavors best. Neither of them cared very much for the overly sweet treats. These contained the ancient but newly popular ingredient called sugar.

As they skipped along the walkway toward home, Benny recited a new poem he had heard today. It was a silly limerick from way back when English was a separate discipline taught outside of communications and languages. He changed his voice to mimic the mythical creature he pictured in his imagination.

Je'Nea grinned down at his bobbing head. She was enjoying his antics. She knew he tried hard to make her happy and she appreciated it. She worried sometimes that he was too attuned to her feelings. She prayed her emotions would not adversely affect him when he reached puberty and began to make other ties. She knew he would be ok. He could be so charming.

Benny skipped and jumped along. He paused and looked at his mother's face, wondering why she had slowed her pace. They were almost home. She was listening to something he couldn't hear, but he could feel it. He laughed and ran down the block. She followed slowly.

Benny bounced up the walkway and threw himself into the woman's arms where she sat on the stoop. He began to play with the shiny baubles in her ears and tried to resist being tickled by her. They were nearly wrestling when Je'Nea walked up. She stood quietly and watched.

"Look mommy! She came back. I told you she would come to see us soon."

Benny was so pleased with himself. He had missed his new friend. He ran up to open the door, hopped up the first flight of stairs, and disappeared around the corner. They could hear him stomping up the next level.

Nedra stood up, her hands buried in her pockets. She was awkward, uncertain what to say first. She looked down at her feet. Je'Nea walked past her and entered the building. She started to close the door behind her. Nedra rushed to the opening.

"Wait! I mean, can I talk to you? Aren't you going to say anything to me?"

"We have nothing to say to each other. Thank you for coming to see Benny. I will tell him you had to go."

A pained look passed over Je'Nea's face, then was gone. She moved to close the door. Nedra stepped onto the threshold.

"Please, Je'Nea. I am so sorry I hurt you. I…I want to apologize, to explain. Please just talk to me. Give me a chance to make it up to you."

Nedra pleaded, hoped it wasn't too late to explain. Je'Nea sighed heavily, stepped aside, let her in, and closed the door behind her. She walked up the stairs silently. Nedra followed. Inside their compartment, Benny grabbed Nedra's hand and pulled her toward his room.

"Come see my room," he insisted. She looked at his mother's sad face but complied.

Once he had shown her all he could think to share, Benny put a small hand on each side of her face as she knelt beside him. He looked intently into her eyes and told her she needed to be nice to his mom. She had the sense that he did not speak the words, but she heard them clearly. He peered into her eyes a moment longer, then smiled and sat down to play with one of his toys.

When Nedra returned to the central area, she found the little boy's mother sitting quietly in one of the memory form chairs. Her eyes were closed but Nedra was sure she was intent on her every move. She knelt beside the chair, reaching a trembling finger toward the woman's still hands. The woman opened her eyes and looked at her, a blank expression on her face.

"Why are you here?"

A simple question, but its coldness threw her completely off guard. This was not the same playful creature she had met that evening not so long ago. She knew she had messed up, she didn't know how badly. Nedra stood up and began to pace. What could she possibly say to this woman now? She had to say something.

"I know I was irrational last time I was here. I should not have blown up at you and I shouldn't have just left like that. I didn't know what else to do. I've never met anyone like you. I don't know anyone like that, I mean like you. I didn't know what to expect. I mean, I thought you were just a nice woman who was being overly kind to me."

"So, I'm not nice and I'm not a woman anymore? What am I?"

Je'Nea folded her arms defensively. Her stare was hard and unyielding. Nedra withered under the weight of it.

"No, that's not what I mean. I mean,-- hell, I don't even know if you're human."

"That's enough! I do not want to hear anymore. I was so obviously wrong about you. I should have listened to Mr. Orin when he warned me about you. I do not even believe my own ears. I want you to leave! Now!"

Je'Nea stood up and pointed to the door. Her fury was more scathing than any words could convey.

Nedra thought heat was coming from the woman's direction.

"Wait, just hear me out. I'm trying to explain as best I can. I didn't think there were any more human Empaths. You just don't hear of it anymore. Since the implants, most people are pretty even tempered. How was I to know you were one?"

Now Je'Nea was angry and disgusted. Was this woman even listening to herself? And she believed what she was saying.

"Why do you think that is? The government decided that was a perfect way to handle so-called 'mental inconsistencies' and 'behavioral anomalies'. Give them an implant; program them to be the way we want them to be. And, hey, we can even track them now."

"That's not true. It's for their own safety. With the implants, we can make sure they don't hurt themselves, and if something does happen, we know how to get help for them."

Surely Je'Nea saw the sense in that. The government only wanted what was best for its citizens. The implants were a saving grace.

"Of course, you Security Agents with your extrasensory devices can spot us instantly. You keep close watch on us, don't you? 'For the safety of the citizens.' Order at all costs, right? Never mind violating the rights of the individual."

Je'Nea sat down in a disgusted huff. What was the point in arguing with this woman? She had been indoctrinated with all the appropriate propaganda for her occupation.

Nedra didn't know how to handle the things this woman was saying to her. She had never imagined anyone could not like the Agents. She'd never experienced any outward distrust before now. In fact, people rarely acknowledged the presence of an Agent at all. They just went about their usual activities, whether one was near or not. Did others feel this way?

"You don't like me because I'm an Agent?"

"Nedra, I have lost my only friend here because he thinks I am fraternizing with an Agent. I like you, or did like you, in spite of the fact that you are an Agent. I guess he was right. An Agent can only be what an Agent is supposed to be. 'Present, observant, and courteous.' Nothing more, nothing less. That is what you would have us believe, right? Never mind that you are the government's perfect surveillance system. You see all and know all."

"You make it sound like we're evil or something. Do people really hate us? Or are you just trying to hurt me?"

Nedra looked distressed. She sat down, her head in her hands. Je'Nea came and sat beside her. As much as she wanted not to, she couldn't help feeling sorry for the young woman. Everything she was made to believe about her role in this society was being challenged for the first time. Je'Nea lifted her chin in her hand, saw the clenching jaw muscles, the uncertainty in her eyes. She regretted being so harsh to her.

"Nedra, you have an identity outside of your job. Don't take it so personally. You do your job well and you are still a sweet person. I have seen you. Off duty, you play with the children; you help people carry heavy packages. You are a model citizen that more citizens should model themselves after. No one hates you. Sometimes people do not always like what the Security Agency does but you are just doing what you are told. It is nothing personal and I am sorry that I made you feel that way. You should be proud of whatever you do. I understand it is not so easy to get into the Agency."

Je'Nea smoothed out the young woman's short hair. Nedra seemed to calm down, compose herself. She tried to smile bravely.

"Thank you for the kind words. And I'm sorry about your friend. I assume you mean Mr. Orin. I thought he was your boyfriend or something like that."

"Oh, no. You could not be serious. He is just a nice man who is concerned for me. He knows I am an Empath as you call it, and he knows people can be very upset about that, not that I go around announcing it, mind you. But like you, some people pick up on it, and they are not always as self-controlled as you were when you found out."

Nedra hung her head in shame. The sarcasm cut deeper than the words could. She tried to apologize.

"Look, I'm really sorry about that. I wouldn't do anything to you. I just didn't want you messing with my head. Anyway, it was obvious he likes you more than as a friend and he did not like me. Did he know I was an Agent too?"

"Not until I told him the night you walked us home. He might have seen you as competition, though. I mean he knows I prefer women, but there was never anyone else. Listen, we don't 'mess' with people's heads. That is not what its like at all. I just sense things, feel things a little stronger than other people do. I cannot read minds and I do not try to control anyone. And I really dislike it when you say things like that. That way of thinking is just a poor attempt to justify all the horrible things that have been done to us."

"I seem to be apologizing for a lot of things tonight. Seeing those images in my head just scared me. I didn't know what to expect."

"What images?"

"When we…when we kissed, you sent… I mean, I *saw* a little girl and her parents. I figured it was you as a child. And I saw myself. At the foster residence I grew up in."

"I didn't 'send' you anything. I can only feel things. I sensed you panic when you pulled away. And I knew your anger and fear. Fear of me."

Je'Nea looked down at her hands fidgeting in her lap. The feelings were still very sharp inside her. She did not want to relive them.

"I'm not afraid of you, Je'Nea, not anymore. I had a lot of time to think about how stupid that was. Even though I just met you, I missed you while I was away."

"Where did you go? At first I thought you were just avoiding the research facility, but then I felt your absence. I was starting to think you would not come back. Benny never doubted a moment, though. He likes you."

"I like him too. I took a temporary assignment on Daiton. Three weeks. I just got back."

Nedra had taken Je'Nea's fidgeting hands into her own. They both calmed down as they talked. Now Je'Nea had a nagging worry and pulled her hands away.

"You were on Daiton? How was it?"

"It was quiet. Very nice there. It's very orderly since the riots stopped. They just wanted to give some Agents a break, some time off. So I volunteered. I needed to think."

"About what?"

"About us."

"There is no us."

"I'd like there to be. If you would give me another chance. I can't deny how I feel about you. I dream about you when I'm asleep. I think about you when I'm awake. I couldn't forget you, and I don't want to. You have touched me in a way no one else could and I felt your absence, too. I couldn't wait to get back here. To see you again."

"Now you are talking like an Empath."

Je'Nea joked weakly, but she avoided eye contact. She was tired. Things were just too complicated.

"You need to know something. About Benny and me. I was on Daiton during those riots. His father was killed there. They caught him and tortured him.

Empaths are not allowed there. It is one of those unspoken but socially enforced things. They do not like us and they do not want us there. Did you notice the scarcity of implants? No one to watch there. Quiet indeed, and very exclusive."

"Was Benny's father an Empath, too?"

"Yes. He sent me away before they could catch me. I was light-years away but I knew he was dying. Benny was born soon after. I think that may be why he is so sensitive, and at such a young age. The few of us who are left developed our abilities after puberty. That is why we do not have implants. They did not see any signs in us when it usually showed up in pre-adolescence. We learned to hide the changes. It is not fair to insert those implants in children and try to change us. Benny is exceptionally gifted already and he will be extraordinary when he fully develops. His father was incredible too. That is why I named him after him. Corben just wanted equal rights for us, and he died for it. I will not let anything happen to my son."

"I am sorry. I always thought the Empaths started the riots. I never questioned why there are none there now. Not even foreign Empaths. I'm sorry about Benny's father and your pain. You must have loved him dearly."

"I did. He and I were best friends. We grew up there together, on Daiton. We both wanted a child, so when the time was right we conceived Benny. He would have been a great father."

Hot tears slipped down Je'Nea's cheeks. She closed her eyes to the blurring lights. Nedra put her arms around her, held her close. She kissed the salty tears, caressing the wild hair escaping from its braids. She bent from overwhelming sadness, and underneath it a growing tingle in her spine. She wanted to comfort this woman, be a friend to her, make up for all the pain she had been through. She was shocked by her intense response to the woman's kisses on her neck. She closed her own eyes and let herself be engulfed by the heat swirling about their bodies. She could feel loneliness and fear, laced with sweeping desire. She could feel everything this woman was feeling. She was like a part of her. It was right.

"Stay with me tonight. Please."

Warm breath whispered against Nedra's ear. She burned as a flame rushed through her body. She looked into Je'Nea's glistening eyes and saw her own desire reflected there.

"What about Benny?"

"We ate before we came home. He's asleep now. In that, he's very predictable. He already showed you his room. Now, let me show you my room."

Je'Nea led her to the door of her sleeping quarters. As the door slid quietly open, Nedra hesitated. She did not want to make anymore mistakes.

"Maybe we shouldn't. I don't want to move too fast."

"Then we should take our time. We have all night."

Je'Nea smiled at her, seductively. She held Nedra's hands about her waist as she slowly drifted backward into the dimly lit room. She looked deep into the woman's eyes, pleased that they showed no fear, only desire.

Enticed by the rhythmic movement of full hips beneath her palms, Nedra followed her into the room.

She was mesmerized by her smoky eyes; they gleamed with a warm light of their own, lightening to a deep molten brown. She wanted to give in to the desire building inside her.

As the door slid closed behind her, Nedra wrapped her arms around this temptress. She was captivated by her body. Firm hips and round bottom. Ample bosom. Plump brown apricot cheekbones. Full luscious lips. A cute but proud nose. And eyes that pierced your soul. She loved the feel of this woman's soft curvaceous body pressing into her own. She loved the warmth of smooth skin against her cheeks. She inhaled the faint scent of her body, infused with a delicate floral fragrance. She was quickly losing herself to sweet sensations sweeping through her own body.

Je'Nea closed her eyes and allowed herself to be held. She had not yielded to anyone since she had left the riots, nearly six years ago. She had managed to avoid the interest of would-be suitors by being polite but aloof. She remained as unobtrusive as possible. She went to work, limited her socializing to only work-related conversation, and came straight home at the end of the day.

She had only recently begun to talk with Mr. Orin. He was a kind man who sensed that she needed a friend. She was surprised one day when he asked if she was an Empath, but she was honest and he didn't seem to mind.

They began to discuss events going on in the news. It was refreshing to meet someone who was not so entrenched with the current propaganda. She tried to ignore and redirect his perceived attraction to her. She decided it was probably because he thought she needed to be protected.

Yet here she was in the embrace of this young woman. A person sworn to protect all citizens, but who had rejected her for being different, now holding her as if she were the most precious thing in the universe. And she gladly surrendered to her.

Nedra's arms were strong, muscular without being bulky. She maintained a healthy body, but she was thicker than the average Agent. She was 5'6", but in no way petite. Her waist was the same girth as her torso and hips.

She liked the fact that she could wear what she pleased without bothering with a chest support garment. Though not exactly flat-chested, she looked androgynous in certain cuts of clothing, especially flowing garments. Still she preferred the baggy body suits that cinched at the waist to slightly accentuate her upper body and her derriere. This was the only true vanity she allowed herself.

Her Agent uniform was a combination of loose-fitting overalls with a loose panel of material that covered the front and back of the wearer to ensure that uniformity and anonymity was maintained. Gender and physical attributes were only relevant to statistical data generated in the administrative offices. She was very glad to be a woman at this moment.

They held each other tenderly, enjoying the feel and touch of their differences. Their passion had not dissipated but only calmed to a steady heat. They each drew strength from their embrace. They seemed to touch more intimately in this stillness than they could in a hurried state of activity. Their bodies began to sway slightly. They were vaguely aware of the lights going out. Then Nedra noticed the faint glow of Je'Nea's skin. She pulled back to look at her.

"You are…kind of shining. Is that normal?"

At this point, she was willing to believe that this woman might be more different than she could imagine. Je'Nea smiled that knowing smile again. She held up Nedra's arm.

"So are you, and yes, it is normal."

Nedra stood back to examine herself. She opened the top of her suit and saw that her entire body was emitting a dark reddish light. As anxiety began to rise in her, she told herself to remain calm. The woman would explain, give her a chance. Maybe it was some strange part of lovemaking for her. She could handle it, as long as it wasn't permanent. Relax.

"You just returned from Daiton, right? It is an atmospheric affect of being on the planet. Everyone experiences it there. I would think your Agency would brief you on something like that. Then again, it is only a minor thing."

"There is nothing minor about having radioactive light coming out of my skin. I was only there three weeks. What is this going to do to me?"

"You are overreacting. It is not radioactive. Your skin just absorbed the natural light waves there. Relax, it will wear off in a few days, no more than a week."

Je'Nea walked over to the bed and sat down, leaning back on her elbows. She watched, amused as the woman rubbed her skin, checking to make sure it was still normal. She could see her clearly in the dark room. Though this was not exactly how she had imagined seeing her body for the first time, the view was no less pleasing.

Nedra had opened her suit to the waist and Je'Nea couldn't refrain from looking at her firm breasts and smooth abdomen. She noticed the scar disappearing around the right side of her belly, and imagined the pleasure she would have tracing it to whatever sweet place it led.

Satisfied for now that no unusual growths had appeared, Nedra looked at her audience. Though the room was completely dark, she could see her clearly.

"Why are you glowing? Did it transfer to you?"

"No silly. I am a native of Daiton, remember? It is permanent for me. It is such a low frequency that it is only visible in complete darkness. Since I am usually in bed asleep by now, my light timer is set to automatically turn off. I was not expecting company tonight. Sorry I did not reset it. Would you prefer light?"

"No. Um, it's ok. I had no idea. This was definitely not in the brief on Daiton. Maybe no one ever noticed. Most people like a little light. I guess if you emit your own, then you don't mind the dark. So you always look like this, I mean in the dark?"

"Yes. It is quite soothing really. Reminds me of home. Happier times."

"Is Benny like that, too?"

"No. Benny was born here on Deronus. No light absorption in this atmosphere."

Je'Nea stood and walked over to a closet hidden behind one of the thermal sensitive panels on the wall.

She took out a thin white garment. She handed it to Nedra.

"Here is something you can sleep in. You can change while I go check on Benny. I know you are tired; and you've had a lot to deal with lately. Make yourself at home." She left before Nedra could say anything.

Nedra was embarrassed. She never lost her cool, yet here she was acting like an uneducated little kid. She had practically undressed in front of this woman, in a most unappealing way. She had again managed to insult her about being different. And she really was too tired to try to rectify the situation tonight.

She wanted to leave yet she wanted to stay too. She put on the sleeping garment and sat on the edge of the bed. It was very comfortable being here. The quiet room seemed to have a calming effect on her and the mellow glow of her skin no longer disturbed her. She allowed herself to relax and waited for Je'Nea to return so she could apologize once again.

CHAPTER TWO

When Nedra awoke, she lay with her eyes closed, listening. She could hear the faint sound of birds singing. Music played softly nearby. She was completely rested and just happy to greet another day. She slowly stretched and opened her eyes.

The room was familiar but not her own. Sunlight washed the pale colored walls and reflected back onto the bed. She sensed movement and looked down at the woman stirring beside her. The bed covers were made of the same material as her sleep garment. However, she could discern intimate details of the sleeping woman's body.

She must have fallen asleep before Je'Nea came back. But how did she get in the bed? And why was this woman lying naked beside her? Did more happen than she remembered? Before she could avert her gaze, the woman opened her eyes and smiled at her.

Je'Nea stretched and folded her arms over her head on the mass of wild hair. She yawned contentedly, looking at her companion. She looked radiant, even in the daylight.

"So you are up before me. I thought you would be a late-sleeper. I guess I should have known better, you being the 'military type' and all. Did you sleep well?"

JeNea began to get out of bed. Nedra tried to stop her. For modesty sake, she turned her head.

"Wait, you're not dressed. I should leave or something."

"Why? My robe is right here."

She stood and wrapped it about herself. It was nearly as sheer as the bedclothes, but sufficiently covered her nakedness. Nedra held her head down, embarrassed. Je'Nea observed this, surprised.

"Surely you are not shy with me. After you undressed in front of me last night?"

"That was different. I didn't mean to, I just wanted to make sure I was ok."

"You are more than ok. You are quite beautiful. It took a great deal of self-restraint to resist such a bold invitation."

"It wasn't an invitation." She became defensive in her discomfiture.

"Unfortunately, I knew that. That is why I left you alone for a few minutes. I did not want to be tempted to do something hasty. Please forgive me for my immodesty. I am accustomed to sleeping nude and sleeping alone. I thought I would be awake before you and no one would be the wiser. I misjudged. I apologize for making you uncomfortable."

Je'Nea walked to the wall near the wardrobe panel and a door opened there. She stepped through the door and it closed behind her.

Nedra got out of bed and began to straighten the covers. She fussed at herself silently. She didn't like that she was getting so bent out of shape over little things like who slept where, and what they wore. She was not like this.

Women expressed interest in her before. She was certainly not new to the game of seduction. Besides, nothing happened. They were sleeping, perfectly harmless. Like old friends. She said she wanted to slow down, be a friend, right? So what was the problem? The problem was that she was not this attracted to her friends and she certainly never slept in the nude with them.

Maybe she still had reservations about the empathic abilities. And this glowing skin thing was definitely unexpected; she would have to check on that. What other little secrets did this woman have? Did she even want to know? Yes, she wanted to know. She just wished she didn't want so much. When she saw her lying there asleep, she wanted to touch her, make sure she was real. How could one woman be so voluptuous, so attractive, so intelligent, so self-assured, and yet seem so fragile? She began to hum "Wildflower". That's what this woman was to her, and she wondered if others could see how unique and beautiful she was.

Nedra went to the concealed door where Je'Nea had exited, and she stepped in when it opened. She quickly covered her eyes and turned around when she saw it was a bathroom, and that Je'Nea was taking a shower. She stammered an apology and stumbled toward the door, but the steam on the pale walls made the door harder to find this time.

"Since I obviously took too long, why don't you join me? Or is that too forward of me?"

"I didn't know this was your bathroom. I thought it was another way out the room. If I could just find the door...."

Nedra's back dampened as Je'Nea reached around her to open the door. Je'Nea's sultry voice was dangerously close behind her, whispering in her ear.

"There you go. You are free once again. Another clever escape from the calculating vamp. Just like the plots in your 20th century Earth novels, yes?"

Warmth and wetness spread over Nedra's body like wildfire. She turned to face the woman inches from her. She smiled coyly.

"No, not at all. Maybe the vamp fell into a trap herself this time."

She pulled the woman to her and kissed her forcefully. She was on fire and she didn't want to escape at all. Her body throbbed as she pulled her damp garment off and pressed the woman's wet nakedness tight against her. They kissed hungrily, tasting the desire ravaging them. Breathless, they pulled apart only enough to safely enter the shower together. Feeling the warm water cascading over their feverish bodies, they savored and caressed and explored each other to near climax.

Je'Nea clutched Nedra's hand to her breast, biting her lower lip, fighting the urge to cry out in ecstasy. Then she froze. She pushed her lover away and rushed out of the shower. Grabbing a thick cover hanging on the wall, she quickly wrapped herself and ran to the door. "Benny is out there," she whispered as she left the foggy room.

Nedra leaned against the cool surface of the shower stall to catch her breath. The woman's abrupt exit left her dazed and frazzled. What was the hurry? How could she so easily disengage from what they were doing?

Nedra grew weak but she composed herself, stepped out of the stall, and dried herself off. She couldn't put on the damp sleeping garment heaped on the floor again, so she just wrapped a thick cloth around herself like Je'Nea had done. She cautiously exited the bathroom, finding the bedroom empty. She quickly put on the body suit she had worn the evening before. As she secured the top, the door slid open and Je'Nea walked in.

"Mmm, déjà vu. Is that what they used to call it?" Je'Nea walked toward her but paused at her expression.

"Listen, I am sorry I rushed out like that. I heard Benny coming and I did not exactly think it appropriate for him to see us as we were. Besides, I sensed you were not completely comfortable with the situation."

"What do you mean? I was all over you. I've never been more excited."

"I know you were excited, but you were reacting too, to my actions. I like flirting with you. I like knowing that I make you flustered. I like feeling your desire for me. And the heavens know I want you. But I must be more patient. And I can be; after all, I've waited a year already just to meet you. I can wait for as long as we need to."

She hugged the woman tightly.

"Now, while you decide whether or not to forgive me for leaving you in the shower, I must get dressed; Benny will be done with his breakfast soon. I promised to take him to the recreation center today. Some of the students from the Advanced School he will be joining this week are meeting there to socialize. He is so excited. I am too, and a little scared. I hope they are nice to him."

"You must think I'm some sort of control freak or something. I don't have to decide if I'm going to forgive you."

"I do not think that at all. I just know you are a very serious person and …well, we were involved in some very serious activities. I would be upset if you had left me…'high and dry' so to speak. Or is 'hot and bothered' more appropriate?"

Je'Nea smiled wickedly, and then momentarily disappeared behind a flash of iridescent material. Closing the wardrobe door, she smoothed the silken fabric over her body, pleased with the clinging effect and the way the lush garnet garment complemented her brown skin color.

"How do I look?"

Je'Nea walked over to hug her pouting lover. Nedra looked into those big shining brown eyes and any resistance melted away. She wrapped her arms around the woman.

"Are you wearing that for me? If yes, you look delicious. If no, then I'm sure we can find something more matronly."

Nedra began to nuzzle her neck, nibbling her way down to an exposed shoulder. Je'Nea shuddered. She leaned into their embrace.

"I am definitely wearing it for you. But if you keep that up, I will not be wearing it for long. Which reminds me," she said, kissing the woman while gently moving from her embrace, "I have never had a need to lock my door. I suppose it would be wise to engage the voice recognition feature, now that I never know when I will find myself in compromising positions."

She began to comb her hair, her tone becoming more serious. The wild locks of hair seemed to defy gravity. She quickly tamed them into a single braid.

"We also must be more mindful of Benny. I will have to discuss this with him. He's never had to share me with anyone. I don't know how he will feel about it."

As if on cue, Benny walked in and jumped on the bed. He looked from one woman to the other, and smiled.

"Are you coming to meet my new friends, too? Mommy says they are going to love me because I'm special. Do you think I'm special, Nedra?"

He looked doubtful. Nedra sat down beside him, pulling him onto her lap.

"Of course, you are special. There is only one Benny, and you are it. That's pretty special, huh?"

She saw relief slowly fill his little gingerbread face. He had the same twinkling brown eyes as his mother, who stood watching them, pleased that they got along so well.

Benny knelt on the bed and started to show Nedra little trinkets he had in his pockets. He pulled out a tiny orb with intricate designs on its surface. Stretching his fingers out flat, he let the orb rest in the fleshy palm of his hand and concentrated. The lines of the patterns began to glow a deep hunter green, then a holographic image of a man appeared. Benny smiled at the image and the man smiled back.

Nedra peered at the image. It was an older version of Benny, but without his mother's features blended in. She watched the image fade and Benny placed it back in his pocket.

"Did you know my daddy?" he asked, collecting his things.

"No. I didn't know him, but I hear he was a good person."

"I think he sent you to help my mother."

Benny climbed down off the bed and began to count steps to the wall. He hopped around and began to count his way back. He was deep in thought.

"Why do you think that? Help your mother how?"

"I don't know. But you will help her when the time comes." He stopped counting. "Mommy, I'm ready to go."

Je'Nea walked over to take his hand. "You are right. I have kept you waiting long enough." She turned back to Nedra. "You can stay here as long as you like. Make yourself at home."

"Actually, I have to go, too. I need to train for at least an hour. And I need some fresh clothes."

Nedra frowned down at her wrinkled suit. She followed them out, Benny leading the way.

"What time are you two thinking of coming back? I could meet you here."

"Why don't you meet us at the center and we can spend some time together."

Je'Nea shot a quick glance at Benny tugging impatiently at her arm. He stopped immediately. He would wait patiently.

Nedra agreed and they went their separate ways. She walked to the nearest shuttle terminal and climbed the spiral stairs to the top, preferring them to the hover lift. There were plenty of passengers waiting by the time the air shuttle arrived. She found a seat near the back, but gave it up to an elderly woman who boarded after her. She stood watching the scenery below as the shuttle zoomed to the next district. She lived three districts over. She liked the changing terrain of this planet.

When she was accepted into the Agency, she had heard that Deronus was still considered a trouble spot.

Since her post here a year ago, she hadn't seen any evidence of trouble. Maybe they said that to shake up the new cadets coming here.

For the most part, citizens kept to themselves. They were polite and courteous, even helpful at times. They were just a little reserved with strangers at first. Once they got to know you as a familiar face, they were much friendlier. She had even learned the names of some of the tenants in her building.

When she arrived in her compartment, she found a text message waiting for her. It was from the Agency. She decided to change clothes and eat first, then deal with business. She was still enjoying the new sensations she had experienced this morning. Waking up beside a beautiful woman and wanting to spend the rest of her life with her was something she would have to process a little more. Was that really what she wanted? She knew the three of them were meant to be together, that it had always been so, even though she knew that was ridiculous. This could have been one morning like countless others, except that she knew it wasn't and was embarrassed by the intimacy of it. She was so comfortable with this woman. They seemed so familiar with each other.

Nedra's past experiences with women had been varied. They might have started out good but something always went wrong in the end. Most were mild flirtations that never went very far. She had become physically involved with only four women in her life. The first two had been too young and too unsure of their sexual preferences. The third one just wanted someone to sleep with when she visited the planet. And the fourth, well she found out that sleeping with one person to make another jealous could cause you to lose both. When Nedra found out the woman was using her to get her old flame back, she promptly excused herself from the relationship. She had to take cold showers for two months after that. It was hard to believe that much passion had been wasted on a silly childhood game.

She hoped with all her being that this time would be different. She had just about given up. But this woman had more than enough little secrets to make her wonder. At least she was honest about who she was, or seemed to be.

After choosing a clean outfit and enjoying a hearty meal, Nedra sat and read the message from the Agency. It was very short and stated that she was expected at an important meeting today. She had to hurry if she was going to make it on time. Luckily the station was on the outskirts of her district.

The United Systems Security Agency district building was constructed of a lightweight polymer material that hardened into a firm, durable but thin shell over a dome shaped skeleton. Inside, the walls provided only adequate absorption of the noise generated in the Security station. There was a great deal of activity today; people rushing through the large central dome and disappearing down curved hallways.

Nedra walked briskly down the far left hallway, maneuvering through a crowd of government officials standing outside the double doors of a large conference room. When she entered the conference room, it was already nearly full. She found a seat and was handed a briefing packet.

The packet contained two small thin discs. She inserted both into her digital viewer and saw that they contained short accounts of events that were being investigated, a list of suspects possibly involved, and images relating to each case. She shifted through the images and listened to the lieutenant's droning voice explain their various roles in the investigations.

One of the video streams caught her attention. She stared at the man and woman walking close, leaning slightly toward each other as if conversing. She zoomed in on their faces. Their mouths did not move except for occasional twitches, but their faces showed undeniable changes of expression. There was something else strange about the image, something not quite right about the background. The trees near the couple looked different from those in the left corner of the image, a difference in lighting. There was a slight change in the lighting on the ground as they walked past the foliage. Slowing the video, she carefully studied the subtle changes. Then it came to her. She was seeing the faint outline of a building that was not really there. Searching through the notes and finding no mention of this, she tagged the image on her viewer. She would have to study these images more closely when she returned home, on a larger screen. Putting the viewer away, Nedra focused her attention on the speaker.

"You are late."

"We didn't exactly set a time to meet. Nor did you specify exactly where this place was. Good thing I have excellent deductive reasoning skills." Nedra playfully tapped her temple.

"Yes, well you are still late. Most of the other children have already left. Benny and I are going home, now. We don't care to be out past sunset." Je'Nea straightened her son's shirt and led him down the walkway. Nedra followed.

"I apologize for not getting here earlier. I know we were supposed to spend some time together. I do have an excuse, sort of."

"Let us hear it then." The woman kept a steady pace, looking straight ahead.

"Well, when I arrived home I had received a message about an important meeting I had to attend. I was almost late for it, which would have cost me serious demerits."

"But you made it on time of course."

"Of course. Then I had to go back home and study the information I was given. I'm still not done with that. It was getting late and I stopped working. I rushed right over."

"How sweet of you to remember us."

"Am I forgiven?"

"Perhaps. Though it may take a little more persuading than that."

"I look forward to the challenge."

Seeing a mischievous twinkle in the corner of Je'Nea's eye, Nedra took Benny's free hand and they walked quietly for a while. She looked down at the little boy, wondering at his unusually sober mood. She glanced inquiringly at his mother who shrugged her shoulders. Joyously, she swooped down and lifted the boy onto her broad shoulders. She looked up and was rewarded by his big snaggle-toothed grin.

"And how are you, my best little buddy?" He giggled and held tightly to her head as she bounced him around in a circle. Je'Nea fussed at her to stop before they both ended up sprawled on the ground. After catching his breath, the little boy began an animated summation of the day's activities. As they turned up the walkway to his dwelling, he became quiet again.

Upstairs in the comfort of their own compartment, Je'Nea kissed his forehead and sent him off to bathe while she prepared something to eat. Nedra helped her put together a light meal. The three of them ate, sharing minor details of their afternoon, then Benny allowed his mother to carry him to his room. She returned shortly.

"Poor thing. He was already nodding when I lay him down. He was really tired out today. But he enjoyed himself. And he made some new friends, his own age." Je'Nea walked over to Nedra and leaned into her arms. She glanced around at the tidy room. "Thank you for cleaning up. I was going to do it after I'd put him to bed."

"I want to help. Besides, you are tired too. Perhaps I should carry *you* to bed."

"I don't think you could even lift me, Hericles. And for the record, I have just enough energy left to be persuaded that I should forgive you for coming late to meet us." She poked a slender finger in her lover's shoulder.

"Oh, yeah. I almost forgot about that. We should definitely retire to the bedroom, then. By the way, it's Hercules, not Hericles." She grinned at the woman's sideways glance. "Mmm, where to start?"

Je'Nea laughed softly as she led her to the large seat in the central area. "Come cuddle with me for a while. I just want to listen to your voice and be close to you." She nestled her head on Nedra's shoulder, breathing in the warm scent of her neck.

"What do you want me to talk about?" She smoothed the woman's hair and kissed her forehead.

"Anything. Talk about you. Tell me stories about your childhood." Her voice sounded so small.

"Me as a kid? That will be a short story. Let me see. 'It was a dark and stormy night...' right?" She glanced down expecting to see a disgusted sneer, but saw only patient stillness. The phrase was too old to be cliché anymore.

"Well, I was an orphan. I was one of those highly sought-after newborns over which families disputed, but I grew past the cute toddler stage before the local adoption agencies could decide who would be the most suitable or lucrative parents. Of course, by the time they decided, I was too old for anyone. Who wants a resident urchin when they could have a newborn to train from the beginning?"

Nedra shifted her hips in the cushiony seat and placed her free arm behind her head. Now that she was more comfortable, she continued her story.

"There were plenty of us so I never was lonely. We were cared for; the commonwealth kept us healthy and provided adequate education to ensure a steady future labor force. We were given all the standard tests and were even trained according to our aptitude for certain skills. If we were fortunate enough to know our own self worth, then some of us managed to break out of the cycle of undesirables. You know the old adage:

orphans begat orphans, kings begat kings. Well, maybe
you don't; it was an old Earth saying."

"What planet were you on?"

"The first home I remember was on Tynre 5, but
we had to evacuate; some strange seismic activity, I
think. If I remember correctly, I was about seven, so that
would place it at the time of the Great Shift. No one
lives there anymore, though it is stable now; too many
superstitions."

"I hear there are beautiful caves there."

"Maybe, but there isn't really any travel in that
area anymore. They moved us to Tynre 9. That was a
harsh, dusty planet; at least, outside the districts. Some
of us would sneak out at night, just to prove we could."

"I can't imagine you breaking the rules."

"Well, I didn't say it was a wise thing to do.
That was really dangerous back then, and really stupid.
One particularly stupid night, we wandered upon some
'Unregistereds'. We thought we were tough, right? But
these people were infamous; they were the threat that
kept us in line. We thought if we could talk to them and

live to tell about it then no one could ever question our superiority. That night changed me forever."

"What happened?"

"That night I decided I would become an Agent. I saw how rude and unruly a people could become with no order. They spoke in a loud jumble, everyone at once. We could hear them but we couldn't understand them. Yet they understood each other perfectly. They laughed at us, mocked us, as if we were the misfits. Then they robbed us. They took everything, including our clothes, and left us in the wind and dust. We were so mortified. How we managed to sneak back in without getting caught I cannot even tell you. We were called the Red Crew for years after that. Our skin had been chafed raw by the dust storms. Of course, it was obvious we had been outside the boundaries of the district, and we were heavily penalized for our insolence. We not only endangered ourselves but the entire community. A way out is also a way in."

"So now my rebellious troublemaker is sworn to protect and maintain order so privileged citizens like me can sleep safe at night. How can I not love you?"

"Do you love me?" A heavy silence followed the barely audible question.

Je'Nea raised her head to look her squarely in the eyes. She studied them intently. "Do you doubt?" she asked, still searching, waiting for the answer.

Nedra broke her gaze, looked quickly toward the door, then down at her lap. "Well, this is only our third date." She knew Je'Nea was still looking at her, but avoided eye contact.

Je'Nea's voice was playful but her demeanor was serious. "Technically, we have never been on a date since we have never spent time together outside my compartment."

"Then let's meet at my place next time." Nedra smiled wryly as she glanced at her.

Je'Nea did not respond. She sat back and closed her eyes, massaging her temples. She was too tired to feel anything else. She just wanted a nice quiet evening, a little time when she could feel sheltered, safe from the constant bombardment of other people's emotional waves. She was unwise to seek shelter in the midst a storm. She sighed deeply.

"What are you afraid of Nedra?" she asked calmly.

Nedra looked at her defensively. "Just because I joke with you that doesn't mean I am afraid of anything."

"No. I do not mean that. I mean, do you know what it is inside you that holds you back?" Nedra started to protest. Je'Nea held up her hand.

"Wait. Before you argue, just listen for a moment. Some people believe that within each of us there dwells a...a spirit...an essence of sorts...something beyond flesh, beyond blood, beyond even cognizant thought. It is what makes us who we are, as individuals, and yet it manifests itself as a greater existence, one that encompasses us all. When you saw those people living outside your district as a youth, you recognized them as 'different than', as 'other', yet you also had a need to identify with them. You yourself were considered an 'other', within the acceptable bounds of a social order. With those boundaries removed, they represented to you a microcosm of the roles that society had imposed upon you. Outside the district borders, you were acceptable in the eyes of your society and these people became the undesirables. Whether by choice or necessity, these people were living in a seemingly lawless fashion. They did not register the conception and birth of their children. They did not submit themselves to the proper battery of tests, no physical and mental evaluations at the appropriate age group. They did not allow themselves to be categorized and implanted with digital tags if need be. They could not be scanned and easily identified as safe or unsafe, balanced or imbalanced. They made their own rules. They existed on their own terms. And they got away with it. When your caretakers found out you had managed to sneak out and return without detection, save for the skin irritations, did they punish you because you disobeyed, or did they punish you because you succeeded? There is something within you that revealed itself that night. And it scared you back into the safety of order. Remember, you said so yourself: the way out is also the way in; therefore, safety is relative."

"Ok, my little philosopher. That is enough for now. I will ponder it and learn its deep meanings, I promise. But now we both need to sleep. You can barely hold your head up."

Nedra's unease during the monologue had given way to concern when Je'Nea had fallen back into her arms while talking. Her voice had grown thin and her body slack, but she continued to speak as if in a dream. As Nedra helped her up and into the bedroom, Je'Nea began to tremble slightly.

"I am so tired. I must tell you what happened today."

"Shhh, not now. Tell me tomorrow, after you rest. It looks like Benny is not the only one who wore himself out today."

Nedra helped her change into a night garment and get into bed. Then she tucked the covers around her and took a thicker cover from a low table in the corner to place over them both. She lay close and held her tightly in her arms. She recognized the signs of extreme fatigue from her professional training, but she had not helped anyone so afflicted; she hoped she was doing the right thing. Without her helmet, she had no way of knowing exactly how to help her, though without an implant, details of Je'Nea's condition would not register so explicitly. She rocked her gently, sang softly to calm her.

"Benny said you were ready, but that your fear would hinder you."

Her voice, barely a whisper, trailed off into soft slumber. Nedra wondered what she meant but did not want to wake her. She lay quietly and slumbered herself.

Later in the night, Nedra awoke from a strange dream. She saw herself running down a long winding corridor that had no ceiling. She could see the sun but she could not feel it. She could hear wind blowing but she could not feel it either. In fact, she could not even feel the impact of the ground beneath her feet. She stopped running and found herself in a vast open field, like a perfectly manicured lawn that stretched beyond the horizon in all directions. She was alone. And she was empty and tired.

Nedra carefully climbed out of bed, mindful not to wake the sleeping woman next to her. She went into the central area and stood near the windows. She opened the shutters and let the moon light shine on her. Looking

73

up past the outer buildings, she could see a pale sliver of one of the two moons that orbited Deronus. She perched on the sill and listened to the night quiet.

Nedra awoke, still tired after working the double shift. Not ready to open her eyes yet, she pressed her face into the pillow and let the cool air on her back awaken the rest of her body. Yawning, she finally opened her eyes. Benny's sad brown eyes stared back at her, his face perched on the edge of her pillow. She started, began to rise out of bed but remembered the thin clothing she wore, and quickly clutched the covers tightly to her body.

"Benny what are you doing in here? You shouldn't just come into Mommy's room like that. Besides, you startled me."

The little boy tried to speak but his mouth began to sag and quiver uncontrollable. Big fat tears blurred his eyes and slid down his cheeks. His small frame shook. Nedra sat up, pulling the thick cover around her body, and reached for him. She glanced behind her, but there was no one there. She looked at Benny's wet face. He threw himself into her arms.

"Hey, it's ok. I'm not angry with you, buddy. I was just surprised. Mommy's not going to be angry either. Benny, where is Mommy?"

"Mommy's gone. Mommy's gone!"

A knot formed in Nedra's stomach. She didn't like this at all. She lifted the little boy's face up to look her in the eye. He tried to explain in choppy words. He broke off in heaving sobs against her chest.

"Benny, tell me where she is. Did she leave? Tell me what you mean."

"Mommy…went to…the store. She said…to be quiet…not to wake you…she would be…right back…but…but …I can't feel her...anymore…she was worried…now she …she's gone…."

She didn't know what to do. If Je'Nea just went to the store, then she would be back soon. Maybe he just got a little scared being alone and came in here until she woke up. She patted his back.

"Mommy will be back soon. And I'm here; I'm awake now. You don't have to be scared anymore.

We'll wait together." She wondered how she was going to get dressed if he was afraid to be alone. She could keep the door open and talk to him while she got ready.

"Mommy is not coming back. She is gone. She is not at the store. She's not in here anymore." He pointed to his small chest, and stared down at it sadly.

Nedra grabbed the bedclothes around her and ran out into the main room. She called Je'Nea's name, looking down the hall and into the other rooms. If this was a prank, it was in very poor taste. Someone would have to be crazy to upset a little child like this or to put him up to something like this just to get a laugh. The knot in her stomach began to ache dully.

"She wants you to take me to school today." Benny followed her with his sad eyes.

"What? Take you to school?" She looked at him incredulously.

"She left a note." He pointed to the table.

Nedra rushed over and picked up the paper. Je'Nea's neat script gave what looked like exact coordinates and instructions to the Mae C. Jemison Advanced School, including the headmistress's name.

There was nothing else to do but comply. She left Benny sitting in the main room while she hurriedly dressed in the bedroom. They left soon after. She could come back and look for Je'Nea after he was safe at school.

When they arrived at the location provided, it reminded Nedra very much of a place she had seen before. Perhaps it reminded her of the orphan residence where she grew up, only this place was more cheerful. Groups of children were playing on various parts of the grounds and they sounded happy. She took Benny through the front doors into the bright hall and to what looked like an office. The woman standing with her back to the door spoke first. She turned and smiled down at Benny.

"Ah, Mr. Sincera, you have arrived just in time. Your teacher will be along shortly to take you to class. Would you please wait with the other children in the activity room?"

She watched as he cast an anxious glance up at the woman whose hand he still clutched. He reluctantly let go, then walked to the other room.

"Good. I am Headmistress Jerika Ano. Thank you for bringing him in this morning. Now, I have a letter for you. This is of course confidential. I was instructed to trust you and I certainly trust the source. I will leave you for a moment to read it."

The headmistress stepped out of the room and disappeared. Seeing no one in the hall to answer her many questions, Nedra unfolded the letter. It was in the same script as the note on the counter. She looked around, saw no one, and began to read.

Nedra-

I am sorry I left without telling you anything. Thank you for bringing Benny to the school. They will take care of him here. Please do not discuss the school or its location with anyone.

There are some matters I must attend to alone. I must insist that you do not try to locate me. I will not be home and your presence there will only raise suspicions.

Trust that I am well. Again, I thank you for your assistance.

-Je'Nea

Nedra refolded the letter and put it in her pocket. As she turned to peer through the door again, the woman reappeared in the hallway. She came into the room.

"I hope that you understand what is being asked of you."

"Do you know where Je'Nea is?"

"No. We only knew that Corben would be joining us today, and that the letter was to be given to his escort. His presence here is confidential. For the safety of all our children, it is imperative that our location, our very existence be carefully guarded. I do hope we can trust you, Ms...?"

"Landier."

"I hope we can trust you, Ms. Landier."

"You can. Benny means a great deal to me."

"As does he to many, I assure you. Now if you will excuse me, I have a school to run. Good day, Ms. Landier."

Nedra walked out of the room, still unsure of what had truly transpired this morning. She checked her chronometer; if she did not hurry, she would be late for work. Unanswered questions swirled in her head on the way to the Agency. She could not fathom why Je'Nea would leave without saying something. If she was in trouble, surely, she could have asked for help. And poor Benny, he was an emotional wreck; why would a mother do that to her child?

Nedra wished she could have kept him with her. He looked so scared, so alone. Being with her would probably have been even scarier; she didn't know the first thing about caring for a child. And what would she do with him when she was working? She couldn't take him on patrol. Who ever heard of an Agent with a kid for a sidekick? What did the other Agents do with their children? They probably had spouses to care for them, or they went to school. Most kids were in school when they were old enough to walk. Boarding schools were common for older children. Why had Benny only recently started school? What about truancy laws? And why the abrupt change to lodging?

Nedra rushed to her locker and donned her uniform, with only minutes to spare before the pre-shift briefing. She hurried into the small conference room and found a seat. Most of the faces were familiar, but a few new ones were sprinkled in the group. She could sense from the tenseness and formality that something big was brewing.

CHAPTER THREE

The squadron leader stood up and addressed the room. His voice was stern, strained. He spoke with uncharacteristic formality. He called the meeting to order then introduced the visitor to his immediate left. Commandant Oslo Ravinow nodded curtly to the audience then commenced with a brief visual presentation.

Nedra watched the surveillance footage with increasing apprehension. She recognized the same man and woman from the video disc, walking close yet talking without words, but they were in a different locale. However, the man looked somehow familiar this time. She focused on the words of the commandant.

"These two are wanted for questioning. Several children and adults have disappeared and we have reason to believe one or both of these persons have information that may assist in the location and recovery of these missing citizens. The footage from Agent visual scanners has allowed us to document meetings between these two suspects, but they manage to somehow elude prolonged monitoring. They seem to disappear before another Agent can pick up their image. They are now our top priority. We must locate and successfully bring in this man and woman for questioning. Your briefing cubes will contain the additional information you will need to assist in this most vital assignment."

The Commandant nodded again in conclusion. An assistant began to pass out the briefing cubes among the agents. Nedra received hers and placed it in her reader immediately. She sat a moment too long as the crowd dispersed. The squad leader called her up to the small group assembled at the head of the room. She joined them and nodded stiffly.

"I notice you have been absent from your quarters recently. Though you are free to do as you please, we are of course concerned for your safety at all times. Have you encountered any difficulties we should know about?" The leader held her eyes for an uncomfortable period of time before blinking.

"No sir. I have been spending more time doing research for a private reason. I am safe at all times. Thank you for your concern."

"You will certainly tell us if you have any difficulty. Please start your shift now. You are dismissed."

Nedra nodded again and turned sharply to leave. As she exited the lobby of the building, she donned her helmet and viewed the information provided in the visor. An alert was posted for the two people wanted. There was also a note regarding suspicious activity in her assigned sector.

Nedra engaged the gliders in her boots and began to carefully but quickly glide through the constant throng of citizens walking by outside. She soon arrived at her designated post and found two other agents searching the area for unusual activity. However, everything seemed normal, from the clear green field to the sparsely populated walkway. The agents nodded to her and glided away. She took a comfortable stance at the intersection of two hover ways, where she could observe transports and foot traffic alike.

Most citizens of the three cities on planet Deronus traveled by foot as each sector was populated by local shops that provided most of what its citizens required to live a comfortable existence. There were specialty shops located in specific sectors, and their items were easily traded to be available to everyone.

The faces of the citizens showed contentment and purpose. That was a sign of stability. That was a sign of order. That made an agent's job easy.

Nedra fulfilled her duty to monitor the citizens and maintain order for the shift to which she was assigned. She declined the offer to take a second shift and headed into the station to remove her uniform. She took a hydracleanse prior to donning her own suit of clothes. She took her viewer and headed to a nearby transport station. As the modest gondola shaped transport glided along above the sector, she perused the viewing cube and read the information provided by the agency.

Arriving at her own home, Nedra sat down in a swing seat and stared at the images of the man and woman again. Something nagged at her mind. She zoomed and angled one of the images. Expanding and projecting a 3D image, she slowly began to see what was so disturbing about the image. She recognized the man.

Though his face was partially hidden by a large black hat, he looked distinctly like the man who was waiting for Je'Nea at the bibliotec where Nedra met Benny and his mother. Perhaps her mind was just adding features in absence of real information.

Nedra placed the viewer down and stood up to stretch. She was fatigued and needed sustenance. She ventured into the small eating area, where she decided to blend several fruit and vegetables together with a small portion of plant-based protein powder. She smiled at the green concoction and took a big gulp. The burst of lemon and ginger pleased her. She walked back into the seating area and stood at a hexagonal portal looking out into a courtyard.

Many agents resided in the living quarters surrounding this courtyard. It was filled with benches and flowering plants. Fruit trees provided shade from the harsh suns during the day and provided snacks at dusk. A few off-duty personnel milled about, reading or tending the communal ornamental and edible plants. She decided to go out and help.

The warmth of the soil was good in her hands. Her long fingers soon were dirty with a bluish tinge, a funny trick of the lighting. She removed unwanted vegetation near the stems of the plants. She carefully loosened the soil for roots to creep out further. She added nourishing fluid to the area as a final task.

Feeling her muscles ache from her efforts, she noticed that dusk had fallen around her and she was alone in the courtyard. She stood up and clapped her hands together to shake off some of the dirt. A plum emerged from a tree blossom just over her shoulder. She reached for it and plucked it from the branch.

She palmed the plum as she walked into her living quarters. She went to the eating area, washed her hands and the fruit, and sat down to eat it, savoring the rich juices flowing down the corner of her mouth onto her chin. A feeling of sensualness flooded her body and a sense of deep comfort washed over her. She thought of Je'Nea then knew with a certainness that she was safe.

She thought of Benny and knew he was safe as well, but she still worried that she did not know the people to whom she had delivered him. Clearly it was some type of boarding school if they were expecting him. But the lack of information given to her bothered her. There was also a strange nagging in the back of her mind. Why and how could his mother leave him with strangers? He did not act afraid but he did not act familiar either.

Je'Nea seemed to be a stable mother but Benny was very upset that she left. It was strange that she would disappear and leave a strict note to her new lover to take her child to school. Of course, that is probably the safest place for him, if she is prone to disappearing. What could it be, drugs, crime? She did not appear to have any of the telltale signs of a drug user. She did have that man, Mr. Orin, who seemed to have some authority over her. Maybe Nedra could dig up some information on him. She could certainly try. It looked like a mystery landed in her lap. And she was game.

Nedra prepared for a quiet night in her own sleep quarters. She already missed the feel of Je'Nea's warm body next to her. That woman was so enticing and charmed her so easily. But she was a trained Agent and would get to the bottom of this. She lowered the lights in her bed alcove, she lay still and embraced the sleep that claimed her for the night.

The next morning, Nedra opened her eyes and took a deep breath. She was well rested and ready to face the day. She took a shower, donned a simple jumpsuit, and headed to work.

Upon arrival, she changed into her Agent uniform, attached her helmet, and walked out the door with a confidence only a seasoned Agent would have. She moved effortlessly through the surge of people on their way to work, her boot-gliders engaged.

She processed the information streaming in her visor. The alert for the two people they wanted for questioning was still there. An alert about the disturbances in her sector bothered her. She had been unaware of any activity but it was possible she had been distracted by her interactions with Je'Nea and Benny.

She thought back and tried to pinpoint the date and time indicated for the disturbances. Someone had an expired medical announcement and had been sent to acquire pharmaceutical updates. That was routine. Another person had high blood pressure and she had suggested they check into the local medical station. Nothing too unusual.

The last alert was not usual. It was an unregistered teen walking among the crowd, whose presence went abruptly undetectable. It had to be a blip in the data. One does not simply cease to be.

Nedra arrived at her sector and began to scan the people as they passed. The usual medical conditions flashed on her visor. She instructed those who needed attention and monitored the rest for the expected mundane readings. Her job was not boring but it could be uneventful for hours.

A child ran by and she advised he slow down and walk in an orderly fashion. He slowed to a walk, grabbed the hand of the nearest adult and passed by the Agent. After walking about three yards ahead, he began to run again. She did not bother to follow. He was just being a kid.

Nedra thought of Benny and hoped he was having fun playing with the other children. They seemed content at the school. She decided to visit the school after her shift ended. She would just check in and make sure he was ok. Perhaps Je'Nea had come there by now.

At the end of her shift, Nedra returned to the Agency to receive any updates or digital cubes mandated during the day. She added two cubes to her reader and set her helmet on a charger for five minutes. While she waited, she read the notes on the reader. The same two people were shown in the alert.

Enlarging the digital file dimensions, Nedra studied the images section by section. There was something nagging just outside her consciousness. What was it? What made these images so profound to her? A man and a woman walking to the end of a block. Trees in the distance, green grass to the sidewalk. Shadows cast along a trajectory. Shadows moving as they moved. The shadows moved. The shadows moved around the green grass as the people moved.

It was the shadows that bothered her. Shadows lay down in an angle according to the light. However, these shadows followed a logic of their own. They did not always lay down in a straight line, There was an imperceptible break in the shadows. It could be an anomaly in the program. Or it could be a clue.

Nedra put the viewer away and gave her mind a rest. She dressed in her regular garments and stepped outside into the heat of the evening. She could taste the humidity in the air. She walked in the direction of the school where she had taken Benny.

She slowed when she had walked a long time. She did not remember the school being far from the Agency or her sector. She stopped and looked around to get her bearings. She sensed she was close to the area where the school was located but she did not see it. She stood across from a green space she had passed many times before. She walked across the street to the sidewalk bordering the space.

She stood quietly and observed. She watched the tree canopies, the wildlife, people walking by. She began to see a pattern to the movements. The wind, breezes she felt, and the way the area responded. She wanted to step into the area but a sign stated Keep Off The Grass. An Agent stood nearby and turned to observe her.

Nedra turned away and walked on to her quarters. She ate. She read. She prepared for bed. She was lonely for the first time in her life. She took a deep breath and tremored as she let it out. She knew now there was something missing from her life. She closed her eyes and accepted the fitful sleep that engulfed her.

Benny knelt down in the sand and drove his toy truck onto the top of the sand mound, making engine noises with his mouth and puckered lips. His thick sandy red afro framed his freckled melancholy face. His companion used another toy to make a moat around the mound. He poured water into the rut and frowned as it was absorbed by the sand. He poured more and was pleased that the water stayed visible. He took a small humanoid figurine and splashed it into the shallow moat. "Foiled again!" he yelled. He looked at Benny, expecting a response. Receiving none, he stood and skipped over to another group of kids, leaving Benny alone.

Lost in his own thoughts, Benny sensed and saw Nedra nearby. He watched as she turned and seemed to be looking at him. He watched as she turned and walked away. A solitary tear escaped the corner of his eye, tracing a dirty streak down his dimpled cheek to land in the corner of his trembling mouth. He licked the salt as he stood up and walked toward the dinner hall.

Benny did not dream of his mother this night. Instead he saw his father Corben fighting, fighting against people who wanted to destroy him. He struggled to get loose from their grip. They pulled him in every direction at once. He shook and twisted his body to loose them but they held on like demons tormenting him.

He could have thrown them all off with a simple flick of his wrist if he set his mind to it. Yet, he refused to save himself. He was the one they wanted, not Je'Nea. As long as they were fighting him, she could escape safely. If they knew about the baby growing inside her, they would kill them both and take it.

Corben eased his body into their clawing hands. He let them pull him into their mob. These were not enemies. He knew each of them, grew up with them. Sat at their dinner tables, ran under the hot suns with their children. Knelt over their sick bodies, rejoiced in their recovery. He was a healer in their community. Yet now he was a threat because the government said so.

The Interplanetary Council of Daiton and Deronus decided that Empaths and people with advanced mental capabilities posed a danger to the well being of its citizens. These mental anomalies could not be adequately monitored. Their abilities did not develop until puberty. Most of these people did not obtain brain implants. Initially, only adults could be chipped. By adulthood, most of these people were able to hide their unique skills. Corben chose not to hide,

The mob dragged him in multiple directions, tearing at his clothes and skin. They threw him to the ground to hold him until the Peacekeepers could get to him. They bound his hands and ankles. They muzzled his mouth in fear that he would conjure some spell on them. They imagined him having all sorts of lurid abilities. To protect themselves, they treated him roughly, bruising and hurting him with no reservations. How easily propaganda took hold in the minds of men.

Benny awoke with a start. He would not cry for his father, or his mother. He understood all too well that each of them had a part to play. He was born into a world different from his parents. His tears were not necessary, not yet. He had a good life with his mother, loving and protected. He grew physically and mentally stronger each day unrestricted. He did not fear. He did not hate. He did not reject anyone.

When Benny arrived at the school with Nedra, he felt comfortable, surrounded by children and adults who were like him. Who felt things like he did. He felt normal.

This sunny morning, Benny rose from bed and folded the sheet and blanket under his pillow. He shoved his cold feet into his slippers and plodded off to the showers, lined up with the other boys in his dormitory. Adults guided them into the bathroom and out the other side cleaned and dressed in their school uniforms, ready for breakfast, then for classes.

Benny's first class was reading in multiple languages. He excelled in languages and made short work of the assignments. He rose through the levels quickly to the teachers' surprise. They gave him increasingly harder tests and he aced them all. He showed less aptitude in social skills.

Daily, Benny asked to see his mother. He could not feel her presence and the teachers explained that she asked them to take care of him for her. He was not satisfied, and began to express his displeasure in disruptive ways. He refused to talk at times. He would not perform his lessons and purposely failed his tests. He would have stayed in bed if it were not for breakfast. Regardless of his maturity in knowledge and mental skills, the teachers had to remember he was a very young child still.

Despite his displeasure, he expressed a calming thought that he could still feel his friend Nedra nearby. He sometimes cried for her. Yet he accepted that he could not see her whenever he wanted, would have to wait for her to see him again. This thought helped him relax enough to complete his school duties.

Though he willed himself to not cry today, Benny was distraught most of the morning. Near midday, he was coming down from a tantrum when the sky literally opened up and air ships fell from the clouds.

The children were frightened and they scattered in all directions, crying and screaming in terror. Teachers tried to round the children up and lead them into the school buildings, into shelter, but chaos ensued.

Doors in the ships opened and uniformed agents poured down surrounding the school. They were dressed in grey uniforms and helmets, sliding down ropes extending from the air ships; they were the dreaded Peacekeepers. They landed and marched into the school, demanding the children be gathered up in the halls, all rooms emptied. The leader walked into the headmistress's office and sat down on her desk. Keepers closed the door behind him.

"Well, well. Here we are at last. You have managed to elude us for years but we finally caught you, Jerika Ano. Headmistress, huh? And what a fancy place you have here. All sorts of violations. Unregistered empaths, missing children, unchipped adults with all sorts of disorders. I don't even know where to begin."

The headmistress closed the book she had removed from the bookcase nearest the door. She stared at the Peacekeeper. She could not see through his grey helmet but she could feel the cruel curl of his lips as he relished the opportunity to renew their acquaintance. She knew him well, knew his despise for anyone 'different' or 'special'. He liked the mundane, the conformist, the easily led. He loved power. Now he flexed this power as his army held her school captive.

The headmistress walked toward the leader and sat in a nearby seat. She arranged the shimmering folds of her lilac skirt around her, smoothing the vintage cut that complemented her figure. She sighed and looked up at the leader of the Peacekeepers.

"Commandant Oslo Ravinow. So you found us. Now what?"

"Now I take your precious protégés and have them chipped like they should have been after birth. You criminals get your due. There is plenty of room for you in the penal colonies. I hear there is a new one on Jupiter. That should be fun with the perpetual storm on the Red Spot."

Headmistress Ano smiled. She remembered the first student that she tutored. He was young, undisciplined, but eager to learn. He did not know how to control the emotions flooding his consciousness. He reacted to them with strange mannerisms, leading to a false diagnosis of schizophrenia.

Jerika Ano was his psych therapist. She immediately recognized his true nature as an Empath. She taught him how to cope with his feelings and tame the constant bombardment of emotions from others. She helped him become a model citizen.

Seeing the need for help in other youth, Ano opened the school. She enlisted the assistance of people who could project images to help conceal the buildings. Built using reflective materials, the construction of the school added to their defense. The student body quickly grew and more empaths joined her to teach and train young students to control and use their abilities appropriately. They existed undetected for years, until now.

Headmistress Jerika Ano knew a terrible fate awaited her and her staff, trauma for her students. She took comfort in knowing most of them would be returned to their families after being chipped and evaluated. However, a few were bound for orphan colonies, those who had been abandoned by their parents for being different. She also hoped that some had escaped when she opened a tunnel below the school by removing the book near the door. She held the book in her lap, <u>Parable of the Sower</u> by Octavia Butler, an ancient Earth philosopher.

Ravinow signaled to the Keepers and they came to escort the headmistress out to a waiting ship. He smiled as the other ships were being boarded by the staff and students under the watchful eyes of the Peacekeepers. Once the school was empty, he boarded his ship and sat across from his prisoner. He stared at her, and refused memories of rejection. He once thought her beautiful, intelligent, worthy of his affections. She would not entertain his attentions and when he found out she was an Empath, he turned her in. But she escaped capture some how. She knew before the agents raided her living quarters. She disappeared from their surveillance system. A near impossible feat.

"Your years are telling on you, Jerika Ano."

"And your position is telling on you, Oslo. Perhaps you should consider retiring. Your health is not as well as it used to be."

"My health is fine. Not your concern. You should be more concerned about those children you've been toying with. Teaching them bad habits, listening to people's thoughts and manipulating their wills. You will be dealt with harshly for your crimes. I will see to that."

"You always were such a kind gentleman."

Commandant Ravinow scowled and stood to retreat to the pilot's cabin. He sniffed disapprovingly and walked away. He would make sure his recommendation was for the harshest of punishment, maximum years to life in a penal colony, perhaps Jupiter or the Cone Nebula.

Jerika Ano closed her eyes. She was emotionally tired. She allowed herself to relax and her mind to stretch out. She sensed the distress of her students. She reached further. She was uncertain but thought she sensed Corben with a teacher. She hoped. She rested.

In a dank cave under the school, a teacher huddled with several children and waited. She held

Benny's hand. She could not hear but could feel the army above them. She waited for an escape route to open up.

Corben had been in his Logics class when his emotions gave way to a full tantrum. His teacher, Inja Pyr, sat beside him and talked him down, while the other students continued to work on their problems, though sympathetic to his plight. They had all experienced similar difficulties when they arrived. They had learned to control their empathy to a degree that made it less debilitating.

The class was being conducted in an outbuilding from the school. Pyr had decided the children could stand a change of scenery today. She took them to the shed and placed several brightly colored logic games around the room for them to solve.

When she heard the commotion outside, the teacher shushed and gathered all her students near the back wall. She guided them through a trap door in the floor, careful to close it back above them. They waited in the earthen cavern until a small door slid open before them.

The class crawled through a tunnel that snaked downward around thick tree roots. After a while, they found themselves in a larger cavern with water running through it, lit only by faint lantern charms the teachers carried about their wrists. Other children and teachers were coming from tunnels around the cavern. These were the remnant of the school who managed to escape the Peacekeepers.

The small group sat on the ground and drank from the clean stream flowing through a bed etched into the rock. Here they would stay until nightfall. Or at least for several hours, according to the timepieces each teacher kept to start and end classes.

Corben was extremely tired and lay his head on his teacher's lap. She rubbed his back to soothe him. Her other students all gathered close around her and she began to hum familiar songs for them. Some lay while others sat with their eyes closed in the dim light and waited.

After a few hours, the children became antsy. They were hungry and cranky, tired of sitting on the cold ground and being still so long. They began to play hand games and tech games on the few readers that they managed to smuggle out when they escaped.

The teachers had been trained in how to keep the students engaged in case of power loss or emergency, but they had not experienced this or tried it before. They decided to pool their resources and use their talents to entertain the children. One teacher, who had very good balance, performed a complicated dance to the sounds produced by another teacher, who created musical tones with his body. Next, a teacher who was a master of deception performed mesmerizing tricks with found objects. Finally, a teacher who could use her hands to make puppets cast intriguing characters on the walls while telling captivating stories.

Slowly the time passed and finally the teachers' timepieces showed a time late enough to expect darkness of night. They gathered their sleepy students and carefully made the climb back up to the surface. Upon reaching topside, they huddled closely, talking only in whispers when necessary.

First thing, they returned to the main school building. Shock registered on their faces at the ruin, with seats turned over, screens smashed. The chaotic scene disturbed the children and they began to cry. The teachers tried to comfort them despite their own sense of dread. They knew they were still in danger there and should move quickly to one of the safe houses set for them if they ever needed them.

The teachers nodded to each other and herded the children into the woods on the south side of the building, farthest from the green fields. They walked through the slender trees, carefully moving over fallen limbs and soft underbrush. Each group of children followed their teacher in a serpentine line, helping each other over the uneven forest floor.

Soon they arrived at a small living structure, its inhabitants already in for the night, with lights shining in the pod windows. They climbed the stairs to the third floor and the leading teacher entered a code in the keypad to open the door to living quarters. They entered the room and found soft cushions on which they could finally rest after their harrowing journey. Still in shock, they slept together that night in the large living room.

The next morning was a late rising. Everyone was tired from the day before. Even the early risers continued to catnap until late in the day. Finally a teacher rose and everyone began to stir. The teachers gathered in the kitchen area to view the well stocked food options. Those teachers inclined to cooking began to prepare a simple meal for everyone. The rest of the adults helped the children get washed up and found unisex clothing of different sizes to accommodate the youth and the adults.

Once clean and fed, the group began to clean up the mess they made upon arrival the previous night. They gathered the items they brought with them from the school, like the timepieces, blankets, cloaks, and dirty clothes, and they placed these items in cleaning solutions so they could be used again. They would be safe there for a little while, but a family unit of unrelated adults and children would soon draw attention. They would need to leave and travel onward to a designated location where they could get safe passage to a place where people like them live in peace. They would need to gain travel to the Exodus colony.

The group stayed for several days, resting, eating and sleeping. The adults prepared bundles for the next leg of their journey. One teacher was designated to venture outside and get a schedule for the next intergalactic journey available. She returned with a few comfort items and information that they would have to stay put for a few more days. Star lamps were in constant use but were a poor substitute for being outside. They took vitamins to supplement their simple diet of proteins and dried vegetables.

On the designated day of their departure, the group was excited but apprehensive to leave their shelter for the unknown. They entered the fresh air and headed for the nearest transport station. They clamored into the first open transport pod that arrived. The children marveled at the structures below them as they zipped along to the intergalactic exchange station.

The docking station was enormous and deafening. The sound of people talking and walking resounded off the dampening panels at turns in the corners of the station. The cacophony of noises assaulted the children's ears and they clapped their hands to the sides of their heads to block it out. As they walked to the farthest bay holding the transport they needed, they became accustomed to the sounds and only noticed when someone spoke to them. They had to speak louder to be heard.

The transport was not open yet and they sat in a corral near the bay where their ship's rusted hulk was docked. They could see the dings and scratches where asteroids had hit the flying machine. Confidence in the sturdy flight of this outdated transport was a bit shaky in the adults. Yet they had no choice and were grateful to be so close to the end of and most important part of their journey.

The adults kept watchful eyes on the children as they wondered around peering at the exhibits depicting the history of space travel. Corben saw an exhibit further down the corridor and moved to it. As he took in each detail of the display, he began to feel them come to life.

Each piece moved in its intended fashion. The tiny people walked around, climbed, and worked at repairing the damaged transport in the exhibit. Doors opened and closed. Passengers peered out the windows.

Corben giggled as the characters performed their roles. He did not hear the sounds of passengers getting on the real transport in the loading dock around the corner where he left his classmates.

After he mentally put the pieces back in place, he turned and a wave of panic hit him upon seeing the other exhibits absent his peers. He hurried to the bay and dropped to his knees when he saw the sealed door and empty dock. He had been left behind. They hadn't noticed his absence and left without him. He was alone in a strange place.

Through his tears, Benny began to hear the bustle of people in a nearby bay. He followed the noise and blended into the torrent of people exiting the station. People of all species and shapes spilled out into the sunlit day. Benny followed a person dressed in vibrant colors carrying a bundle of cloth. He guessed this was a merchant carrying his wares. Soon he arrived in a boisterous outdoor marketplace and he quickly blended into the crowd. He hoped no one would question why he was out and about alone.

Benny walked around surveying his surroundings and taking in the new sights, sounds, and smells. He had lived a sheltered life with his mother, only going to the bibliotec, the recreation center, and home. When he began school, he had not been there long enough to go to the museums they occasionally visited. This was his first time out in the world, and on his own. He was excited but terrified. He tried to keep his composure and appear calm. His life depended on it.

As he walked from booth to booth, aisle or triad, Benny sensed the stretching of the day and a rising panic that he had no shelter or protection to which he could return. He did not know the way back to the deserted school and did not know where the remnant of students were headed. He found a shadowy corner in the crook of an archway and sat down with his head on his knees. Despair overtook him and he began to sob quietly.

An annoying tingling sensation began to nag at the back of Benny's mind. It was like a memory he had forgotten and he didn't feel like trying to remember it. He shook his head fiercely to drive it away. It persisted and seemed to grow stronger. He wiped his face on his sleeve and peered out. Something familiar caught his eye. The stoic form of a Security Agent was visible at a vantage point near him. He arose and moved away to another section of the marketplace, careful to avoid detection.

As Benny moved deeper into the vending arena, the stalls transformed into produce. There were all kinds of food there. Benny's stomach grumbled, acknowledging he was hungry. He did not have any currency. He wondered if a vendor would give him something to eat. He moved closer to a stall of fruit and started to speak, when the nagging sensation in his head increased to a sharp image of Nedra. He swiveled his head from side to side but did not see anyone familiar.

Benny moved away from the produce stall and began to walk quickly through the aisles. Perhaps this was a warning, a sign of danger, or was he projecting what he wished for. He squeezed his eyes closed then opened them again as he bumped into a merchant.

The vendor grabbed him and spun him around to see if he was stealing. He struggled to get free but the vendor held him firm with three arms. The ash grey creature emitted a gravelly sound as it spoke. Benny did not fully understand the language but sensed the meaning. He shook his head no and held up both empty hands. The creature let him go but gave a menacing growl and frowned.

Benny backed away. Six steps into his retreat, another hand grabbed him, pulling him backwards into a shadowy corner. A hand clapped over his mouth and muffled his scream.

CHAPTER FOUR

Benny looked up. Nedra knelt down and whispered for him to be quiet. The Agent in the market had detected the disturbance and moved closer to the stall where the vendor had grabbed him. The creature had returned to business and revealed nothing to the Agent. As the Agent returned to a favorable viewing point, Nedra took Benny by the hand and exited the market. She took him to a less crowded area and he recognized a green growing area leading to a living sector.

Nedra and Benny entered the sector and rode the lift up to the 5th level. The octagonal lobby sported seven solid colored doors. Nedra rushed to the white door and dragged Benny into her living quarters, the soft swoosh of the door closing behind them. She began to pace while the child sat on the stiff furniture. She bit her lip as she allowed herself to think about what she had just done. She should have turned Benny in to the Agent as a lost child, and as a known Empath. Instead, she brought him to her home. Now what?

Benny reached out a small hand, a sign of peace. He wanted her to be calm, to be ok. He knew her discomfort was because of him. He curled up into a ball and began to cry again. She stopped and looked at him, so small and scared. This was not the happy little boy who sang about spaghetti. What caused him to be alone in the marketplace? She stopped worrying long enough to kneel down at his side and hug him. He thrust his arms around her neck, needing that connection, needing to feel protected even for a little while. Nedra sat on the floor and held him in her arms, rocking him until they both calmed down.

"We are safe here. Now tell me what happened to you? How did you get here? Why aren't you at school?"

Nedra remembered looking for the school and being unable to find it. She wondered what happened and waited to hear. She hoped she had been mistaken and looked at the wrong place.

"They came to our school and took everyone away. They dropped from the sky and grabbed the other children. We hid and ran away in the ground. I got left."

"What do you mean? Who dropped from the sky? Where are the children and teachers?"

"Grey Agents. They took everyone inside, but no one is there now. We hid from them a long time and went somewhere else, then I got left by the ship. I came outside and you found me."

At the thought of it all, Benny began to tear up again. He still sat in Nedra's lap. She could feel him shaking in fear. She told him she would protect him, that he was safe now.

"Where is my mother? I can't feel her."

Nedra looked at Benny, holding him at arm's length. She searched his big brown eyes, uncertain of what he meant or might say. She asked anyway.

"Benny do you know what happened to your mother? Do you know where she went?"

"No. I felt her leave, go away fast. She did not come back. I can't feel her anymore. She is not here."

Benny pointed to his head. He looked Nedra square in the eyes. He wanted to know why. He had never been alone before, his mother always close by. Now he felt deserted twice, first by his mother, then by his schoolmates. What if Nedra left him too? He could not bear the thought and clung to her desperately.

Though she did not fully understand, Nedra sensed his apprehension and held him a little while longer. She heard his stomach growl and asked if he was hungry. He brightened up a bit at the prospect of food. He followed her into the kitchen area and watched as she prepared a meal for them both. They sat and ate in silence.

Nedra cast furtive glances at Benny during their simple meal. She could not believe that he sat there in her living quarters. She could not believe she was breaking the law, just by having this small child in her home. She was aiding a fugitive. She was breaking her oath as a Security Agent. She was unsure what to do. Should she turn him in? Should she try to protect him? What if someone started asking questions or turned her in? A lot of what ifs ran through her brain. She finally let out a long sigh. She knew what she was going to do. What she had to do.

She prepared Benny for bed and tucked him into the covers on her sleep shelf. She lived a minimalist life and did not want a bed taking up space so she had a single unit installed in the wall. She would sleep in the living room. However, Benny begged her to stay with him. She curled around his small body on the shelf and soon fell asleep herself.

The next morning, a tone sounded and awoke Nedra. She gasped; it was time to get ready for work. She would have to leave Benny here while she was away. She showered quickly and prepared a meal for them both. She left him eating, with instructions to remain quiet during the day. He understood.

Nedra arrived at headquarters, donned her uniform, and took her seat for the morning briefing. The leader showed images of the school raid, with the headmistress in custody. She recognized the woman she met when she took Benny to the school. They were assured the students were safe and being prepared for matriculation into mainstream society via institutions designed for parentless children. Nedra knew what that meant: brainstem implants and orphan homes. She refrained from showing her feelings.

Though she did not have an implant, Nedra remembered her own time spent in similar institutions for the parentless. Depressing, dejected times, punctuated only by the poignant surety that no one wanted you. She remembered the few friends she made. The mistakes she made. She remembered her fear when they slipped outside city limits into the harsh wind and barren land beyond. Her fear when approached by the Unregistereds, who lived or were exiled out there.

The Unregistered were thought to be a mix of creatures with humanoid characteristics. They covered their bodies in rags from head to toe and only their eyes were visible. These were squinted against the sands blowing in the wind. They grabbed the kids and searched them, stripping them of anything of value, including their outer garments. They left them near the city shield and disappeared into the subterrain as quickly as they appeared. Nedra and her friends sneaked back into their home, their skin rubbed raw by the sands. They told no one of their experience and nursed their own wounds.

Nedra held a small relief that Benny had escaped this fate. What would happen to him now, she was not sure. As she prepared for her shift, she listened to the talk around her. She heard three people talking about the raid. They boasted about the children and teachers being easy to capture, herded like animals with fear in their eyes. One person whispered that the leader had a personal interest in the headmistress and spent several minutes alone with her. They laughed as they speculated on what occurred during that time. Nedra grabbed her helmet and headed to work.

When the day shift ended, Nedra was relieved and conversely nervous about returning home. She buried her head in her viewer but kept her ears perked for anything unusual. She rode the lift to her floor and paused a moment before opening her door.

The place looked exactly as she had left it. It looked deserted. It sounded empty. It bothered her. She called out Benny's name to no answer. She sensed panic rise as she searched the small living quarters for him. No sign of life anywhere. She stood in the middle of the first room and listened. She knew there was no way Benny would leave. He had to be here and there were few places to hide in her minimalist quarters. No place except…

Nedra looked in the nutrition area again. This time she opened the cabinet doors. She searched each one and found nothing unusual or out of place. She stood there, listening, thinking. She knelt down next to a corner cabinet and opened the door closest to the corner. She whispered Benny's name again. He whispered back, "Yes."

Relieved, Nedra sat on the floor and asked Benny to come out. He refused. She asked why. He said he was scared. She said ok, he could stay there a little while longer but she expected him to come to bed soon. She left the door open and rested her back against the adjoining cabinet. She talked to him and assured him that she would protect him and they would find his mother. She sang a popular song to him and hummed until she was tired. She excused herself to prepare for bed. When she returned, she held out her hand inside the cabinet. His small hand grabbed onto hers. She could still feel him shaking. She gently pulled him out of the corner of the cabinet and hugged him.

Nedra awoke the next day and returned to work with the intent to find out more information about the raid and about Je'Nea's disappearance. She listened more intently at headquarters and on the street. She was posted in Je'Nea's region and she hoped there would be some talk.

People generally ignored Agents and carried on their conversations without interruption. This was a good way to know if trouble might be brewing. Agents held their posts in an area with good visibility and listened.

Nedra heard some buzz about Empaths being used for research, especially in the science and technology fields. Word was they did not get implants because they could be used for technical advancements. People were afraid they might use their powers to escape. Nedra knew that once the Agency deemed you to be a threat, they did not allow you to escape. People who were threats to society were taken to work camps, often on another less inhabited planet.

Nedra sensed that likely happened to Je'Nea if they caught her. She needed to talk to Mr. Orin. He was the only lead she knew. After her shift ended, she returned to headquarters to change into her clothes then headed back to the sector to gather information.

First, Nedra planned a visit to the bibliotec. She entered the top section where the children's collection was located. There was a different person manning the section. She did not recognize him. She asked about the previous librarian. He said she quit. He mused she had been an intergalactic spy because she kept to herself. She even refused to go out with him several times. Suspicious.

Next, Nedra went to the housing sector where Je'Nea and Benny lived. She walked to their floor but the door was locked. She could hear no sound beyond. A neighbor saw her and said they had not been seen in a while. She left the premises, hoping to find Mr. Orin.

The recreation center was located within walking distance of the living sector. Nedra headed there. As she entered the oblong building, she spied the dark figure of Mr. Orin standing near a group of people. She walked toward him. He was in deep conversation with another man, and did not seem to notice her. When she reached to tap his shoulder, he turned to face her and deflected her arm as he nodded to the other man walking away. His moustache bristled. His dark eyes pierced hers.

"No need for that, young lady."

"I was looking for you."

"You found me. How may I help you?"

"I am looking for Je'Nea. I can't find her."

"I have not seen her. I cannot help you."

"Yes, I think you can. She may be in danger."

Mr. Orin started to turn away, but this statement stopped him. He looked disturbed then regained his composure. He considered his next words carefully.

"I assume you know her well enough. If you do, then you also know why she is missing."

"I do know and I suspect she was found by us."

"She was not "found". She turned herself in."

"Why would she do that? What about Benny?"

"Benny was safe and to keep him safe, she turned herself in. However, he is not as safe as she thought. He has not been located. I suspect he was "found" as you put it."

Nedra had a pang of guilt about withholding information but she did not trust this man yet. What if he was fishing for information? She played along.

"Why do you say that?"

"Of course, you know his school was raided."

"I did hear that. Usually the children are returned to their parents. If they can't find Je'Nea, then they will take care of him until they do."

"Indeed, I'm sure they will. I must leave you now. I have another engagement."

Mr. Orin did not have patience or time for this woman's misinformation. He was certain she knew something but it was not clear what. Obviously, an Agent would know the nature of the school and the reason for the raid. As well as the fate of the children. He turned sharply and exited the center.

Nedra thought she heard a snicker and turned to notice a group of older people sitting across the way, playing several games. Their movements seemed coordinated, play and counterplay. They did not talk. No chitchat or banter. Nedra found this strange and had a suspicion why. She did not know any of the players and did not think it wise to interrogate them.

She left the center and returned home. She had to take care of Benny. She had to keep him safe. She did not like leaving him alone for so long. She was thankful that he was quiet for now. What would happen when he gets bored?

The next day, Nedra returned to the same sector and went to the recreation center. She found Mr. Orin there, sitting quietly in a chair, as if waiting for something or someone. Nedra sat down beside him and waited for him to speak.

"I've been expecting you. Je'Nea turned herself in to the government. However, she refused to cooperate with their questioning. As punishment they are transferring her to a penal colony in the Cone Nebula."

"Cone Nebula? There's nothing there but dust and radiation. That can't be."

"It can be and it is true. They want her to help them in research, using her skills. She is very talented. So is little Corben. That is why she tried to keep him safe at all costs. Now he is missing."

"How do you know all this?"

"I have my sources and I will not reveal them. There are allies. People who do not agree with the way certain people are treated. We try to help in any way we can. Are you an ally, Agent Landier? Do you know the whereabouts of young Corben?"

Mr. Orin's dark eyes flashed across her face, seemed to pierce her mind. What did he want from her? Could she trust him? How did he know so much? Was any of it true?

"No. I don't know anything about Benny."

As if on cue, Mr. Orin stood, smoothed out his dark garments, and walked away. Shocked at his abruptness, Nedra paused a long moment before she followed him outside. When she exited the door, she did not see him. He had disappeared into the crowd of citizens walking about.

Nedra returned home to find Benny in his same hiding place in the corner of the cabinets, out of easy sight. She coaxed him out and they ate a comforting meal of spaghetti. Both of them were lost in their own thoughts about the recent changes in their lives.

Nedra had to figure out a way to keep Corben safe but find his mother at the same time. The only person she knew who could help was Mr. Orin and she wasn't sure she trusted him. Yet, Je'Nea seemed to trust him to an extent. She needed freedom to travel and keep Benny close to her. She would have to take some time off from work.

As if sensing Nedra's distress, Benny touched her cheek. She looked at him and smiled. He smiled back. She noticed his adult teeth were starting to peek out from the gums. He would not be snaggle-toothed for long. He was growing before her eyes. He expressed a wisdom and understanding beyond his years.

"I can help. I can find Mommy."

Nedra knew he was right. He could find his mother quicker than her snooping around would. She would have to take him with her. She just had to figure out a good reason to go to the Cone Nebula. No one went there by choice, except traders and thieves. She needed a ship.

CHAPTER FIVE

Dust and steam rose and clouded the air around rusted but intact machines. Clanging of metal on metal echoed through the haze. Pale skin peeped out of the torn mechanic suit Selera Dorn wore. She had been working on her ship for most of the day and was as disappointed in her progress as she was yesterday. It cranked but still idled like a mewling cat. Throwing down a big wrench, she climbed out of the metal cavity housing the tired engine. No use wasting time, she would have to find the missing part to get it running again.

Selera grabbed the hand extended to her and jumped onto the floating dock. She squinted at the person standing there, the suns nearly blinding her. She shook dust from her wayward hair and pushed past without a word. She entered her modest living quarters, leaving the dock gate open for the person to follow. Adjusting to the low light, she squinted again at the person, now seeing a familiar female face, and shocked to see a kid in tow.

Nedra held Benny close behind her, shielding him behind the folds of her unisex clothing. He peered out with curious eyes, knowing this person would not harm him but cautious just the same. He knew Nedra would protect him at all costs. He would protect them both.

Selera clapped dust off her mechanic suit before plopping down on an old amorphous seat. She seemed to surround herself with antiquity, or at least old Earth stuff, like the bean bag on which she now lounged. She eyed the visitors and gestured, indicating they find a seat too.

Nedra moved some glossy papers stapled together and made a space for herself and Benny on an old beat-up sofa. She recognized many items in the converted hangar. She smiled despite herself at the Yoda toaster machine. Her gaze fell upon the mechanic again.

"You have eclectic taste."

"I have good taste. You should remember that. Though we did not last very long, you and I. But no harm, no foul. What brings you back? Still single?"

Nedra squirmed slightly at the last question. She remembered their brief relationship ended amicably. She did not plan to revisit it. She ignored the question and explained what she needed.

"We need passage to the Cone Nebula and a return trip. If I recall correctly, you traded there occasionally. I need to retrieve a package and exit quickly, preferably undetected. Discretion is required."

"How sweet. You thought of me. As you can see, my ride is down at the moment. Sorry, can't help."

"I can ensure your 'ride' gets all the parts it needs to return to peak performance. You will be rewarded generously."

"There is nothing in the Cone Nebula worth exposing a kid to radiation. You have the wrong person. Perhaps in my younger, stupider days."

"I sense you have not aged much and have never been stupid. I can transfer currency to you immediately. When can we leave?"

Selera's face flashed red at the thought she could be bought. She snarled and stood up. She towered over Nedra and the kid.

"Look, you have the wrong person. I have to get back to work. You can let yourself out."

"I do not mean to insult you. You need your ship running again. I can help you with that. I need your help, too. We can come to some sort of agreement. You are the only person who can help us."

Selera stood still and peered into the pleading eyes of this woman and child. What could they possibly need in that nightmare of a place? She did not want to be responsible for anyone getting caught in there. The average being wouldn't last long with that degree of radiation. She could not imagine a reason strong enough to expose a child. Yet, she knew enough of Nedra to know she had already considered the dangers before asking.

"Ok, I'll take you there. I cannot stay long and you will have to move quickly to get a ride back. If I am detected, I will have to leave without warning. You understand this. There can be no tarrying. Quick in and out. Get your package and get back to the ship immediately. I will not be responsible for you --or him."

"You will find that I have already transferred the funds to you before I arrived. Thank you. How soon can we leave?"

"You knew I would say yes. How?"

"Benny knew. I suspected. How soon?"

135

"Two days. Be here early morning."

"Agreed. Until then."

Nedra took Benny's hand and they exited the hangar, walking toward the center of town. Selera watched them until they disappeared from sight. She shifted some papers and found a viewer, tapped in a few codes, and gasped in surprise at the amount in her personal funds. She grabbed an oversized shirt to cover her mechanic garb. Now she could get all the gadgets she needed and wanted. She was like a kid in a candy shop. She shimmied out the door into the bright sun light.

The parts shop was a conglomerate of rusty old and shiny new parts. All kinds of metal objects littered the vast warehouse. Dust hung in the air, suspended in the streams of daylight coming from the skylights above.

Selera moved slowly but deliberately through the piles, searching and surveying each piece she needed before placing it gingerly into her shopping basket. She knew what she could afford and was frugal to maximize the haul she could buy. She needed to make sure she had sufficient spare parts as well as additional parts to accommodate the dangerous environment of the Cone Nebula where they would be traveling. Why anyone would want to go there willingly was beyond her. There was rumored to be a penal colony there, only the worst of the worst were sent there. She hoped to steer clear of that area. Besides, if it existed, it would be heavily secured and restricted anyway.

Selera looked over the collection of parts in her basket again. She picked up two adult multi-layer aluminum insulation suits, and even found one small enough for the kid. She was sure they were enough, but she grabbed a couple more microparticle filter masks just in case. At the register, she hefted the heavy basket onto the conveyer belt and the automated but antiquated robot scanned the whole lot, spitting out a plastic ticket showing the total and the remaining balance. Selera bagged her goodies and sauntered giddily out the door.

The noonday sunlight was blinding after being in the shop so long. She had spent at least two hours in there, not hard to believe given the erratic arrangement of items. She could have shopped at a more modern store but she liked the fact that this old shop carried hard to find parts and specialty items not commonly sold elsewhere. Not to mention their policy of discretion.

Besides, her ship, her baby, used specialized parts. She custom-built it that way. There was no other ship like hers and none could out-maneuver the little scout vessel she had salvaged from a junk planet years ago.

That's about the same time she met Nedra. Cocky and still green, the Security cadet was also subtlely attractive. Selera saw her in a local drinking hole and ordered her a complimentary drink. Nedra raised the glass in thanks. Selera took that as an opportunity to walk over and start a conversation. They seemed to have a lot in common and soon the flirting began. By the third drink, they were heading to Selera's hangar for more serious communication. The evening was passionate and progressed to an entire weekend of lovemaking.

They dated for a few months then Selera noticed Nedra began to drift away as she advanced in the Security Agency. Before long, their relationship had cooled considerably. Then Nedra announced that she preferred to be alone. She moved to another sector and they had not seen each other for years since--until she appeared at the dock with a kid. Selera wondered if he was hers, but refrained from asking.

The relationship with the scout vessel lasted considerably longer. Selera poured herself into revamping the little ship she called Baby. She repaired and customized the engine and vents, and everything in between. The ship was a snug two-seater with a jump seat and tiny cargo hold. It was fast and well equipped, complete with cloaking system and photon weapons. Baby was her pride and joy. She tried to keep it in tiptop shape and ready to ride at a moment's notice. Just lately, some bad decisions resulted in low funds when her ship needed a good tune-up. Though Selera hated to admit it, Nedra's visit proved to be most opportune.

The day of their departure, Nedra arose early to prepare. She packed sparingly, but included an extra tunic that was baggier than she usually wore. Benny would have to wear his only outfit, one she had located at a thrift merchant, one that did not look like school garb. The remainder of her pack consisted of water, anti-radiation drops, particle masks, and dried snacks.

Wide-eyed, Benny watched Nedra move about the living unit. He knew how important this day was and sat quietly so as not to distract her. He pointed to things she seemed to forget, accepting her nod as sufficient thanks. In his palm, he held a small stone object, a heart with an engraving on it. His mother had given him this gift recently when he started having disturbing dreams of his father. She explained the changes he was going through as best she could to a five year old. The message on the heart said "To thine own self be true." It reminded him to be and to like who he is. It reminded him that he was special and loved. It helped him stay calm in most situations. He kept it in his pocket at all times. It calmed him now as he watched Nedra pace the room, checking off a mental list of to-do's.

Finally, Nedra lifted the small pack onto her back. Benny appeared beside her and she took his hand. They walked out of the small living quarter for the last time, together.

The transit carried them from sector to sector until they reached the outer edge of the city. They exited the transit station and walked through the warehouse zone until they reached the hangar where Selera resided. The place looked deserted. It was too early for regular activity to start. The suns were just rising. It promised to be a bright day.

Selera sat in the cockpit of the ship, checking gauges and readouts. In her peripheral, she saw Nedra and Benny approach. She waved them onto the ship. Nedra strapped Benny into a jump seat in the cargo hold. She sat in the empty seat next to their pilot. She took a deep breathe, exhaled slowly. She turned her face to the pilot and nodded.

The ship shuddered as Selera engaged the engine. It whirred to life, a barely audible sound as it backed away from the dock. Once clear, the ship hovered a moment then shot into forward motion. Pressure inside the cabin increased to near uncomfortable levels to protect their bodies during transwarp speed travel. They were on their way, for better or worse.

Several hours later, the small scout vessel appeared on the edge of the Monoceros constellation, at the horn of the Unicorn. The ship travel slowed as Selera maneuvered around the triple star system and tried to avoid black holes and stars forming. Space debris bombarded the ship hull.

As they entered a cloud of dust, visibility decreased to pitch black. Exiting the cloud, the ship's view was filled with a menacing dark crimson and gold plume. They had arrived at the Cone Nebula. It looked even more terrifying than telescope images had depicted.

Nedra's heartbeat increased, fear gripping her soul. She began to think this trip was a mistake. She glanced behind her at Benny, whose eyes were big with uncertainty. She remembered why she was there and resolved herself. Quick in, quick out. Then they could leave.

Selera nudged the ship's engine and zipped through the nearest side of the columnar cloud. She squinted her eyes, searching for a safe landing site. She could see the rough outlines of an old trading post and some sort of colony. She set the ship down in a particularly hazy spot and engaged the cloaking system. She sighed a short breathe of relief. Turning to Nedra, she gave some last instructions.

"You will have to walk the rest of the way. Try to enter without being detected. I did not see any parameter security but that does not mean there isn't any. Get your package and hurry back. I cannot afford to be discovered here; old acquaintances with old grudges and all. I will wait one hour, then I have to move. You have one hour, understand?"

Nedra nodded yes and unbuckled Benny's seat strap. She hefted her pack onto her shoulder and took his hand. They both donned the suits and the helmets with oxygen converters. They exited the ship and began walking as fast as Benny could manage toward the old trading post.

The ground was hard and uneven, though some spots were soft sand that gave with their weight. They walked carefully through the hazy atmosphere, mindful to take deep breathes at regular intervals. Within minutes, they arrived at the trading post.

Beings of all shapes, sizes, and compositions moved around them, mostly ignoring them. Though they attracted an occasional glance here and there, Nedra and Benny seemed to go unnoticed. Nedra stopped at a busy trading stall and listened to the chatter. Without her Security Agent helmet, she had to rely on her knowledge of languages to interpret the many conversations swirling around them. Benny appeared to be listening as well. When he tugged her hand, she knew he was not listening so much as he was feeling for his mother.

Nedra leaned down and Benny whispered in her ear. He could vaguely feel someone is distress, but could not identify anything familiar. They would have to follow his lead if they were to find his mother.

They exited the far side of the trading post and headed toward the colony. About halfway between the trading post and colony, Nedra spied a security detail. She dropped down behind a craggy rock formation. Surveying the terrain, she saw an entry on the side of the rock wall that did not appear to be guarded. They made their way toward it, moving stealthily from crag to crag.

On closer observation, Nedra saw the perimeter was secured by a roaming guard. She timed his return to the entry. They could make it there before he returned if they ran for it. As soon as he turned the rocky corner, Nedra and Benny sprinted to the entry. Nedra noted that Benny was surprisingly fast, his feet barely touching the ground. They entered into a dark hall of sorts, stopping only long enough to catch their breath and plan their next move.

Nedra saw a figure approaching and she felt a pang of fear. However, the figure turned and disappeared down another hall. Nedra positioned Benny behind her, but he rejected the move and came to stand in front. He would lead them. They moved quietly to the other hallway and peered inside. It was a small chamber with a staircase leading below the rock surface.

Benny placed his hand over his small chest. He could feel anguish and despair permeating the air. He rushed to the stair just as a figure entered the hall.

"Halt! You are not authorized to be here."

Nedra's heart dropped where she stood still in the shadows. She was frozen with fear and could not make herself move to help Benny. She watched in horror as he slipped down the stairs, followed by the figure. In a split second, Benny was gone and their whole plan was destroyed. How would she ever find him in this rock prison?

When the figure disappeared down the stairwell, Nedra regained faculty of her limbs. She moved to the stairs and peeped down. A short staircase and hard ground below greeted her. She would have to follow them and try to save Benny. She descended the stairway as quietly as possible, expecting someone to grab her at each step. Reaching the next level, she saw no one in the small room and a dark doorway leading out.

Nedra leaned against the wall and listened at the opening. She could hear nothing. Despite her fear, she entered the opening, keeping her back against the wall. The next room contained a number of prisoners latched by iron rings set into the rock. They looked dirty and hollow-eyed, devoid of any hope at escape. They made no sound and barely looked up at her. Those that did look, quickly looked back down.

Nedra saw another doorway, dark like the first one. She rushed to it and exited the room of prisoners, only to find herself in another such room. The next doorway led to yet another room of prisoners. In this room, there was another stairway down to the next level. A red light glowed from below.

Nedra eased herself down the stairs. At the last step, she paused, listening. She could hear chatter coming from some distance. The room itself was empty, except for the glowing rouge fumes swirling about her. She saw two doorways leading in opposite directions. She walked to the one from which she could hear talking, and something else. Muffled screams.

CHAPTER SIX

Yakob Orin stood before the narrow closet and removed his dark tunic. His black hat hung from a peg on the wall. He stared at his reflected image inside the closet, pale skin drawn tight across his chest where burn scars puckered and merged like deserted streets on a Dutch island he once visited. Though his emaciated frame showed signs of abuse, his sharp eyes scanned the environment like roving laser beams. He missed nothing and no one escaped his piercing gaze.

After donning a lighter tunic, in color and fabric, Mr. Orin turned his attention to his evening meal. He gathered cheese, bread, and fruit to the small round table. He chewed slowly and contemplated the disturbing occurrences of the recent week.

An illegal school for special needs children had been raided by the Security Agents. Several teachers and students were missing. A woman rumored to be an Empath was taken into custody in connection with the raid. An unidentified man and woman were announced as persons of interest in the case.

Mr. Orin suspected there had been a secret school for children with special abilities. He dreaded the possibility that the alleged Empath might be a person he knew. And he knew himself to be the unidentified male wanted for questioning. He managed to elude capture so far and warned his compatriots to lay low as well. Questioning often led to sentencing by the Security Agency.

Why would anyone be searching for him? He was an old man who kept to himself mostly. He occasionally went to the local Community Center to play a game of Acquisition with like minded people. Perhaps that was it. The like-minded people. People who saw nothing wrong with others who had special abilities. People who believed in the motto "live and let live". Perhaps he was too liberal in his thinking, too careless with his choice of acquaintances.

Yakob Orin had always been a carefree boy. He remembered running through the meadows, wading through streams, lazing in the grass on the old farm his father owned. He grew strong and tall, worked the fields when he was older.

In manhood, he had an easy smile and a boyish humor about him. Until he was detained for loitering while waiting for a train during the New Reconstruction Period. He was incarcerated and farmed out to the mines around the planet. One cold morning, in a fit of rage, a bully guard threw a pot of hot coffee at him, burning his thin shirt and thinner skin. Then he was sent to planet Daiton.

There he earned his freedom. A heavy price he paid, he compromised his conscience to fight and round up rioters. Though he wielded his baton and taser sparingly, he was responsible for several captures of would-be escapees. These were subversive people who disregarded the rules of society and endangered children by refusing to have them tested for deadly diseases and infirmities that could undermine the positive medical and technological breakthroughs that made life… well, better.

Later, he learned that the riots had been started by the so-called Peacekeepers, a special group of Security Agents, highly trained in deadly force techniques. These agents raided a peaceful commune of Empaths and differently-abled people, forcing the children onto a ship to be taken to a camp. The adults believed correctly that the children would be used for experiments and the adults would be forced to submit to implants in their cerebellums to suppress their abilities. In a show of dominance, the Peacekeepers killed many of the adults and the orphaned children were taken away.

Remorseful of his part in the Riots, Yakob Orin claimed his new freedom and moved away to another planet. He settled on Deronus, an idyllic planet with two suns, secure city walls, and a new transit system. He chose a humble living pod in a quiet city and began his new life. His only social outlet became frequent visits to the local bibliotec and the community center. Nearly a lifetime later, he found himself caught in a tangled web of trouble again.

advanced people or their allies. He considered himself to be an ally. The people who saw through the thinly veiled attempts of the government to control its citizens were those very people it sought to control the most.

People who showed signs of chronic diseases and disorders were quickly identified and chips were implanted in their cerebellums. These chips were readable by Security Agent helmets to "assist" in keeping citizens safe, to note irregularities in body rhythms, and to obtain medical attention at a moment's notice. Infants and children who showed signs of "abnormal" mental abilities were also chipped, to quell these tendencies. To date, there should be no more abnormalities. Failure to have your children properly assessed was punishable by law.

Of course, in every society there are citizens who do not agree with the policies and practices of their governing body. On Deronus, there was no exception. Some people preferred and managed to keep their children "natural".

Yakob Orin met a few of those parents and even some of the adults who still retained their natural abilities. He had an ill-gotten ability to identify these people and swore himself to secrecy. In fact, he purposed to protect them in any way he could. When he met Je'Nea and Corben in the bibliotec, he sensed they were exceptional. He befriended them and made it his personal mission to protect them with his life. They accepted his friendship and shelter, though Je'Nea kept a little distance between them. He understood this as her survival mechanism and did not stress the issue.

Now that both Je'Nea and Corben were in danger, Yakob acutely felt his impotence in helping them. He could not have foreseen her plan to sacrifice herself and did not suspect the Agents knew about the school. Even he did not know about the supposedly safe haven, though he was not surprised given he did not face the same dangers his friends faced on a regular basis.

Yakob contemplated his next move. He would not yield to the Security Agents. He believed that the only way to aid his friends would be to find and rescue Je'Nea. His mind turning like cogwheels in a fine tuned chronograph, he hatched an ambitious plan. Convinced that he had only one slim choice, he prepared himself for bed and turned off the lights.

Nedra's spine stiffened at the sound of the muffled screams. She could not tell if they were adult or child. Either option terrified her. She had to know if it was Corben, the possibility of his capture shooting shockwaves of guilt to her system. She placed her hand on the neon panel to open the door. A barely audible swish and she was confronted with a scene of chaos.

In a large cavern deep inside the nebula, red gases swirled and debris floated in the congested air. A pair of scientist type personalities manned a console lit up with all sorts of readouts and dials. Across from these genderless beings, a woman was strapped to a gurney. It was her screams Nedra heard, emitted from behind a rigid face mask that forced her mouth closed and her eyes to remain open. Images of atrocities from history projected in the air in front of the woman and she responded with panic, from the images as much as from her bondage. The woman was clearly an Empath and the images of pain and despair heightened her already raw emotions.

Nedra slipped into the room unnoticed. She pressed her back against the wall and shimmied to a shadow cast by unused machinery. She crouched and racked her brain for a solution to free this woman.

Noticing a scattering of pebbles at her feet, Nedra grabbed them up and tossed them out the still open door. As hoped for, the lab coats turned and shuffled out the door to investigate the noise. The door closed behind them and Nedra sprinted to the gurney. She released the straps and caught the weakened woman as she collapsed from the holds.

Nedra hoisted the frail, unconscious woman onto her shoulders. On a prayer that nothing could be worse on the other side of the room, she moved toward the darker end. There she found a small door. Opening it and preparing for the worse, she found it was an exit to the outside. She half carried the woman up the narrow staircase to the surface.

Nedra could hear klaxons sounding at the discovery of the missing subject. She hastily removed the face mask and gasped. Standing before her was an unexpected shell of a woman.

The battered headmistress of Corben's school looked at Nedra with a panicked and anxious expression. She had endured untold horror since the school was raided. She stumbled over her words but managed to whisper a hurried name and location. "Je'Nea, Red Room, save her!"

Nedra nodded. She told the woman to go with the escaping prisoners and she would be able to get away. She watched her join a group of escapees running toward the trade posts. She did not look back; she knew she could not help in her weakened state.

Nedra knew she had to go back in the same way she had exited, because the other side of the compound would be full of enemies by now. She ducked back into the open entrance. She hid along the dark walls and eased back down to the red zone where the torture chamber was located.

Three other doors stood along the walls of the cavern. Nedra knew one of them led out the way she first came in. The other two were unknown. She crept toward the first one and carefully opened it. A man slumped in the corner. She helped him stand and showed him the way out.

The second door was hard to open. Nedra pushed and pulled but it would not budge. She braced her shoulder against the edge of the doorway hoping the full brunt of her weight would move it. She stood back and studied the door and its surroundings. She noticed a slight indention in the wall. Curious, she touched it with her pinky finger. The door immediately swooshed open. Inside the tiny room, a woman lay curled up in a fetal position. It was Je'Nea.

Nedra rushed into the small chamber and helped Je'nea up. She was weak and half delirious from torture. She fought to move away, crawling further into the corner. Nedra spoke calmly to her, assuring her that she was safe now. Je'Nea finally looked at her, comprehending. She pushed her away and clawed her way up the wall until she was upright.

Battle worn and weary, Je'Nea stood before her lover. Her hair had been shorn off and she wore torn dust-stained garments. Nedra was relieved to see her again. Yet, it was short lived as she blurted out that Corben was somewhere lost in the bowels of the nebula.

Je'Nea shored herself up and took charge. She pointed Nedra in the direction of the exit. She demanded she hurry to the nearest outpost and wait, while mother would hunt for child. She knew her keen connection with Benny would help her find him quicker than Nedra's bumbling around in a dangerous environment.

Without waiting for consent, Je'Nea ran out the other exit, avoiding the guards who had already abandoned their posts to search outside. She allowed her heightened senses to lead her to her son. As she encountered prisoners, she used her heightened mental alertness to free them and pointed them to freedom. Small groups of freed people ran from the unguarded exits toward the outpost where Nedra would be waiting for them. She would negotiate passage for them on ally ships already docked on the outskirts of the trading posts.

Sensing Corben's location, Je'Nea made her way to the far side of the compound and burst through the door of a lab, where she found him surrounded by guards with drawn batons and tasers. His small body looked bruised and the site of him in danger raised the "mama bear" mentality in her.

Je'Nea screamed for the guards' attention as she threw herself into the midst of them. She began to fight ferociously, thrashing each guard as they approached her. She shielded Corben behind her back and moved purposely toward the wall, breaking the circle of

159

enemies one by one. She sensed that Corben was using his mental abilities to ward off the guards and she led them to an exit. With all her strength, she thrust Corben out the door and turned her full attention to fighting the increasing number of guards.

Je'Nea willed Corben to escape and he followed the freed prisoners as they ran to the outpost. She allowed the guards to capture her again and writhed with the electricity zapping through her body. Unbeknownst to them, however, she was not weakened by the currents, but instead strengthened by the adrenaline. In a burst of energy, she forced the attackers off of her and escaped through the doorway out of the compound. The dazed guards could not follow.

Je'Nea ran toward the outpost and arrived just as Nedra lifted Benny into her arms to carry him to her ship. She donned a heavy coat and helmet to disguise herself and followed them to the location of the ship. When they reached the place that Selera's ship was supposed to be docked, Nedra stopped short. The ship was not there.

Thinking they were stranded, Nedra grabbed her comm and attempted to make contact with the ship. No answer. She tried to stave off panic. She knew guards would be coming soon to scour the area for them. She tried again to contact the ship. No answer. She looked at Je'Nea, disbelief on her face.

Je'Nea moved toward her and pressed her forehead against hers. She emitted a calming glow. Benny grasped both their hands and squeezed. For a moment, the air around them seemed to hum. Je'Nea broke the connection and advised Nedra try once more.

Crackling sound emitted from the comm in Nedra's hand. The voice of Selera came through with instructions to meet her at another destination near by. They gathered their strength and sprinted to the new rendezvous.

Unfortunately, the sounds of the comm were picked up by the guards, too, and they followed close at the prisoners' heels. Taser blasts surrounded and narrowly missed them as they ran. They dodged around rocks and stones, careful of their footing on the treacherous ground.

Through a hazy fog, the scout ship appeared, hovering above a craggy outcrop of rock. The ragged pair of women and small boy made their way to the ship. They threw themselves into the open bay door and the ship zipped away from the surface, exiting the nebula while dodging asteroids and debris. The passengers barely managed to fasten themselves into the harnesses along the walls of the tight space before they entered warp speed.

Nedra strapped herself into the co-pilot seat and let out an exhausted sigh. She looked at the pilot with gratitude. The pilot looked back with seething anger.

"You brought a prisoner onto my ship!"

Nedra's face fell in surprise. She thought their mission, though messy, had been a success. She searched her mind for a reason to explain this outburst of anger.

"Well, yes. I told you I needed to retrieve someone."

"Uh, no. You didn't. You said you had to get a package and get out quickly. This is not a package and it was not quick. I had to move to evade detection from swarming guards. Now I am breaking all sorts of laws because you brought a prisoner on board. You did not tell me that!"

"Ok, maybe I forgot to say a person but does it matter?"

"Yes! It matters! Let me decide which laws I break! Besides, this ship is already crowded and now another person. Who is she anyway?"

"This is Je'Nea, Benny's mother. I had to rescue her. I had to get your help anyway I could. I didn't think you would agree to help if you knew I was going there for someone."

"I see. And this someone is your lover, yes? I can practically smell it on you. You used my ship to rescue your lover? Are you crazy?"

Nedra grabbed the bottom of her seat as the small ship dipped violently. She was aware of the explosion of emotion she had caused by not thinking through this turn of events. She only thought of the first person she could convince to help her and that she had to move quickly. She did not think of the dynamics involved in bringing these two aspects of her life together.

Je'Nea sat silently, too exhausted for a confrontation at the moment. She noted the conversation, but deemed it wiser to let them hash it out. She resented being spoken of in the third party. However, she was just grateful to be free again.

Je'Nea conserved her energy, sensing she may be needed all too soon. She made certain Corben was safe and was able to comfort him by her nearness, their mental connection restored. She tried to rest while they traveled. She ignored the heated conversation between the pilot and Nedra as best she could, noting the tension stemming from an obvious past history.

The argument ended abruptly as they fell from warp due to ringing sirens and a warning voice declaring damage to the ship. Several enemy ships appeared on the tail of the little scout vessel, weapons blasting. The ship shuddered as the pilot flew evasive maneuvers while trying to triage the damage.

Selera yelled for Nedra to take the controller in front of her and fire back at the gaining ships. Nedra, unsure, began pushing the button she saw on the controller. She whooped when one of the bursts hit an enemy ship. Her excitement was short lived as the weapon fire was returned. She persisted, becoming more confident with each successful hit until one of the enemy ships crashed into another and they both exploded.

The force from the explosion pushed the little scout ship further out of reach. Selera was able to engage the warp again. The small ship disappeared from the scene without further damage.

They traveled in silence. Each woman was lost in her own thoughts. Corben slept. The ship flew through space toward their planet. Little did any of them know the ripple effect their escapade had on their home on Deronus.

Word spread like a virus throughout the cities on Deronus that prisoners had escaped the penal colony in the Cone Nebula. The reports said that multiple ships departed with an unknown number of convicts. Some were suspected to be heading to the planet, causing a panic among the cities.

Those who knew the true nature of the penal colony secretly cheered. They gathered in community centers to plan their next move. While the government was rattled by the escapes, the groups of mentally gifted people and their allies prepared to shelter their newly freed brethren. Some rallied to protest the government's unlawful detainment of its citizens. They would make sure people knew the truth at last. People were being held against their will and used for experiments because they were different.

Yakob Orin hurried into the community center and sat at the games table with his friends. They discussed the best ways they could be of use. Some would harbor the returning citizens. Others would go to the Security Headquarters and protest. They would need to make signs like those seen in old Earth footage before heading there.

Yakob Orin offered his services. He knew the most about the Agency's maneuvers concerning Empaths. He would stay hidden in plain sight by disguising himself as differently from his usual appearance as possible. He would infiltrate the Agency and don a uniform to obtain intel. He would report back to a Council of Elders that included members from the other cities. The Remnant, as the renegades called themselves, was officially activated.

CHAPTER SEVEN

Security Agents swarmed into the cities. They were ordered to keep the peace at any cost. Confiscate any kind of subversive propaganda people may be posting or passing out to others. Capture any persons found disturbing the peace or who fit the profile of the escaped prisoners.

Citizens panicked and were uneasy with the increased security. They hurried along the streets, casting furtive glances at the Agents but avoiding direct eye contact. Many did not leave their living quarters at all, only venturing out in extreme emergencies. They no longer were safe.

The threat of escapees in the cities caused fear and discontent. The rumors of Empaths among them caused people to distrust each other. The increased presence of Agents did little to ease the tension. People were afraid of being detained and disappearing. They were encouraged to report any suspicious activity immediately. Even the slightest suspicion could be reported and cause one to be taken away by Security Agents.

In this heightened atmosphere of fear, Yakob Orin slipped quietly into a nearby Security Agency and stole a uniform from an absent Agent. He retreated to a restroom and donned the clothing, tossing his own into a garbage chute leading to an incinerator. Though it fit loosely on his thin frame, the suit allowed him the incognition he desired.

Daring to hope no one would suspect him to be in the Agency, he appeared in the briefing room with his helmet under his arm. Make up by one of his compatriots hid the gaunt features of his face. He stood in the back of the crowded room and listened to the briefings. Now armed with the same knowledge the Agents had, he donned his helmet and moved amid the throng leaving the station for their shift.

A hand on his left shoulder, Yakob slowed and fought back panic in his throat. The Commander asked him to wait a moment. As the stream of Agents thinned, the Commander asked if he was ready to return to the field after his injuries. Yakob nodded emphatically and voiced his affirmation, praying his voice did not sound unusual. Luckily, the Commander did not know the

Agent well enough to know his voice. He patted Yakob on the back and sent him on his way. With a sigh of relief, Yakob exited the building and hurried to catch the nearest transport.

Standing at the back of the transport, Yakob marveled at the amount of information his helmet provided for each of the passengers. He also marveled that it did not pick up any anomalies for one of the passengers he knew was an Empath and that he was not detected as such. He avoided looking at any one person too long, but turned and faced the rear window of the transport so that information would not be recorded. He noticed the Empath exited at the very next stop, a place he knew was not the man's living region.

Yakob continued on his journey to an undisclosed location. He knew only that he was to look for an advertisement for the latest available infant chipping device. The idea disgusted him so that he nearly missed the sign.

He exited the transport at the appropriate stop and walked the distance he was instructed to travel. He waited on a corner near an open field, reminiscent of another area he had promised to protect with his life. This one was just as important, if not more so. He waited for an unknown person to arrive and take him to his final destination.

While he stood and waited, Yacob observed the thin stream of people passing by. He read their scans. He watched their movements. He wondered if one of them was his rendezvous person. A person approached him and he noticed there was practically no read out for him. He did not shy away from the helmet but approached him boldly.

"I am here for you, Yacob Orin. Come with me."

Yacob turned and followed the muscular young man with the healthy read-outs. He followed him into a narrow alley between two one-story buildings, emerging to reveal a second story camelback house. They climbed the metal stairs to the second floor and entered a door barely covered with chipped painted.

Inside, his helmet was ripped off his head and he folded over from a violent punch in the gut. He was shoved onto a cold metal chair and tied tightly to the surface, then dragged into the center of the room where a bare lightbulb dangled from the low ceiling in an otherwise dark room.

Still winded from the punch, Yacob tried to answer the questions asked of him. A deep voice asked personal questions in rapid succession, demanding he answer or suffer descriptive acts of violence. He answered as quickly and as honestly as possible. He knew the routine. This was a scare tactic from the old world, thought to be the most efficient way to abstract information from a potential enemy. He hoped it would end as soon as they knew he could be trusted. He tried to remain calm.

After the deep voice was satisfied that Yacob was an ally and not an enemy, the muscular man came and untied him. He shook his hand and received a glass of water. The muscular man introduced himself as Cherge Den and asked that Yacob follow him to another room.

The inner room was more cheerful, filled with natural lighting from the skylights, and outfitted with a wrought iron table and chairs. In one chair, a portly man sat drinking tea from a delicate China teacup and eating a scone from a matching saucer. The table was set for three. Yacob and Cherge joined the man.

"My name is Paul, leader of this faction of The Remnant. You must forgive our awkward interrogation and understand the delicate position in which we find ourselves. Security Agents are trying to infiltrate our ranks every moment. Your disguise has the unfortunate trigger of setting us on edge, while simultaneously helping us gain much needed intel about the Agents. We apologize and thank you for being brave enough to abscond one of their helmets."

"I accept the apology and am glad to be of service. I am an ally and can be trusted to perform any missions you may require of me."

"Yes, Yacob Orin, your reputation precedes you. We know about your past service during the Riots and your rededication to protecting two of our own over the past few years. It is unfortunate that Je'Nea and Corben Sincera fell into the hands of our enemies."

"I take full responsibility for their capture. I should have been more diligent in keeping watch."

"Nonsense. Je'Nea is a fully grown woman and chose to sacrifice herself to save her son. Corben is our most gifted asset. The teachers who escaped the raid lost him, not you. Nevertheless, it is rumored that he may have been rescued recently. As you may have heard, escapees from the Cone Nebula will be arriving soon and will need our protection to avoid recapture."

"I heard the news broadcasts. The propaganda to make citizens afraid is clearly an Agency endeavor."

"I agree. Your success at obtaining an Agent helmet will help us expose the Agency for what it is: a totalitarian dictatorship."

"That will be difficult. People genuinely believe the Agents have their best interest in mind. They already know the helmets are used to scan their vital signs for rapid health intervention. How will we prove otherwise?"

Up to this point, Cherge had remained silent. Now he shifted in his chair and looked at Paul. Paul nodded, while offering a buttered scone to Yacob. Yacob accepted and poured himself a cup of hot tea. Cherge cleared his throat and turned his attention to Yacob.

"The citizens of Deronus know the Security Agents use their helmets to scan for health issues. They know chips are implanted in people's brains to help control malaises. What they do not know is that Empath children are being tagged for experimentation purposes. They do not know that adult Empaths are being tortured and used to develop techniques of mind control. They do not know that the President of Deronus is no more than a figure head being controlled by Commandant Oslo Ravinow, a ruthless dictator in the Peacekeepers Agency, to which the Security Agents are beholden."

"Whew. Are you sure the citizens can handle the truth? Most of them believe Empaths were wiped out long ago, at least since the riots. There will be no love lost for any who exist today."

"True. However, this is a benevolent society and if they knew Empaths still exist, they would not want harm to come to them, especially children under the age of chipping. It is illegal to chip a child under the age of five years, except in emergency situations, due to the inherent danger of causing irreparable brain damage. If they knew the government did this anyway, they would be outraged. If they knew Empaths are living peacefully among them, they would be less likely to fear and would balk at any injustices committed against them."

"What about the people living outside the cities?"

"If citizens knew these are peace-loving Empaths, they would condemn the government for excluding them. They would demand these people be accepted into society as they are, possibly without being subjected to dangerous chipping."

"You have high minded hopes for the people of Deronus. I am not convinced they will embrace Empaths as readily as you believe. They have been programmed to believe quite the contrary. How do you plan to show that Empaths are harmless? We don't really know all that they are capable of doing."

"I see you are playing 'devil's advocate' as they said in the old world. Your concerns are valid. I propose we expose the government's misuse of people first. Once everyone knows the government has been lying to them, they will be more accepting of our message about the benevolence of Empaths."

"You have my pledge to help in any way. I do ask that I be informed of the situation in which you may find Je'Nea and Corben Sincera."

"Yes, your self-appointed wards, who managed to escape your protection. Rumor has it they were captured by the Peacekeepers. A great loss, as both Mother and child were particularly gifted. The child especially was to be protected at all cost. However, he did not arrive at the safe colony with the other children from the school. We can only hope he is still alive."

Paul motioned for Cherge to take Yacob to the central room where the Remnant soldiers were preparing to receive and protect their brethren who would soon arrive from the Cone Nebula prison. Yacob observed the arrangement of rooms around a central courtyard. On the grounds below, people practiced movements reminiscent of the old martial arts movies Yacob liked to watch in his younger days. He never knew anyone who could duplicate those moves and his heart raced at the prospect of learning them.

Cherge smiled at Yacob's excitement, a common response of new recruits. He led him to a room with a narrow bed. He indicated for him to enter, explained when his training would begin, and left him to rest. Yacob lay on the bed and closed his eyes. He would need his strength.

CHAPTER EIGHT

The students and teachers arrived at the Exodus Colony to find they had lost Benny along the way. Inja Pyr, his young teacher, fell into a pall funk because she had been directly responsible for his safety. Her inexperience and fear had hindered her ability to account for all of her wards in an appropriate manner. She had allowed the children's constant need for attention to draw her from her direct mission to ensure Corben was protected at all times.

Now Pyr stood before the Council leaders, feeling their barely controlled wrath. Corben possessed an advanced skill set that had not been seen in a youngster his age nor in any adult Empath since his father on Daiton. Yet she had managed to lose the one child on whom all their hope depended.

Though many on the Council thought another Empath would be best suited to protect Corben, they conceded that a well trained ally would draw less suspicion. Now they debated the error of their thinking and questioned Pyr relentlessly. She sensed the tension increasing with each inquiry.

Inja Pyr hoped the Council would agree to send her out again, this time teamed with an Empath, to find the boy. She was sure he must have been separated from them while waiting for the second transport. The thought of him being alone for so long frightened her. She hoped against hope that he was able to remain undetected by the Security Agents. The likelihood of this was slim at best. Time was against them.

After much debate, the Council leaders came to a conclusion. They must send Inja Pyr back out to Deronus to search for young Corben. An Empath would accompany her on her search. She had a short window of opportunity to look for the child and recover him safely.

A young muscular male entered the chamber where Inja Pyr waited for the Empath who would help her find Benny. She stood and shook his hand. She exchanged unnecessary pleasantries with him. His serious demeanor melted to reveal an easy smile, but quickly returned to a stern look.

"I am Cherge Den and I will help you search for Corben Sincera. Let us get started."

Without waiting for a reply, Cherge turned and left the room. He led Inja Pyr to a small transport vessel that would carry them back to the intergalactic exchange station. Their search would start there and widen as needed.

As Pyr and Den walked through the exchange station, they observed people moving anxiously with furtive glances, while avoiding true eye contact. The partners searched each transport bay for signs of the lost child. They questioned patrons, in the slim hope that someone would remember or recognize the little boy. Their efforts were unsuccessful. This was to be expected given the amount of time that had elapsed since Pyr was last there. In fact she and the other teachers had made every effort to remain incognito during their wait in the transport bay several days ago.

The search team walked down the hall leading to the transport bay from which the students had departed. Cherge Den commented on the exhibits and stopped to observe them. He could feel a slight vibration at the one depicting transport repair. Sometimes an Empath could sense the change in particle assembly of an object that had been manipulated by a person with telepathic abilities. They left behind a sort of signature on the objects they "touched".

Den was sure the miniature objects had been moved around by a telepath. He also knew Corben was rumored to possess telepathic abilities along with his empathic nature. Inja Pyr confirmed that she had observed these abilities in young Benny at school. They checked the bay again for signs of the child. Their search yielding no clues, they turned their attention to the nearest exit, suspecting this would be the next logical path the child would take.

The exit yielded to a packed dirt road leading to an outdoor market. Colorful cloths fluttered in the warm breeze. Venders called out their wares, seeking to entice buyers to their booths. All sorts of textiles rested in woven baskets. This part of the market waned into food booths packed with fresh exotic fruit and vegetables, fragrant herbs and spices, and healthful plants.

Inja Pyr and Cherge Den slowly walked through the market aisles, seeking signs that Benny had been here. They knew the trail would already be cold but this was their only option, to try and find the same path the child would have taken. They asked merchants if they had seen the child, to no avail.

The market ended at a tall stone building with arched walkways at the ground level. The darkened enclaves served as convenient rest areas out of the heat of the twin suns. Pyr and Den explored the many areas under the building.

Cherge Den thought he felt a possible signature in one of the archways nearest the market but could not be sure. They walked on, seeing a living quarters pod complex ahead. They explored the area surrounding the living pod including the little garden. Inja Pyr remarked on the bounty of purple fruit hanging on the young trees in the garden. They sat briefly on a bench to rest, while Pyr enjoyed one of the purple fruit. She felt a rush of joy as the juice ran down her chin. She wiped her mouth on her sleeve and they proceeded to enter the living pod, hoping to question owners of each occupied pod unit.

Pyr and Den arrived on the third floor where only three units existed. One was locked but yielded no answer. A neighbor was exiting a second unit and Cherge Den stopped him with a simple question.

"Have you seen anything unusual lately?"

"Actually, yes. The woman who lives in that unit must have brought home a little boy one day. She usually goes out daily, to work I assume, and some evenings she works in the garden below. But she has been holed up in her unit for the last few days and now she does not answer her door. I figure she left to return the boy. That happens sometimes when an arrangement doesn't work out. He looked a little wild in the eyes. I only saw him once though, as they were leaving one morning. He was dressed in ill-fitting clothes. Other than that, I don't know anything. I try to keep to myself."

The man raised his eyebrows briefly, then turned to take the lift downstairs. Inja Pyr and Cherge Den were sure this neighbor had seen Corben. Den could perceive a vague sensation of telepathic activity, but without breaking into the unit, he could not be sure. The question was where did they go from there. They decided to return to the Council to disseminate the information they had gathered. They would likely be given directions once they were debriefed. They turned their attention back to the transport station and their small vessel.

CHAPTER NINE

The small scout ship felt nearly claustrophobic with the hostility bubbling between Nedra and Selera. Nedra conceded that she should have informed Selera of the fact that they were rescuing a prisoner and, more importantly, that the prisoner was her current love interest. However, she knew that it was less important now that the rescue had been successful. Selera did not feel as certain of the success as her ship was now damaged and they exceeded the maximum weight of cargo with so many passengers, a load it was not intended to carry.

Je'Nea huddled in the back of the ship with her son Corben curled in her lap. She did not take part in the argument, knew it was best to remain silent. She was grateful for being rescued and for being reunited with her son. She also knew that the hardest part of this battle was before them.

Once they landed back on Deronus, Je'Nea knew the Security Agents would be waiting to take their freedom away again. They would have to be careful to avoid capture. She hoped she could contact Mr. Orin for help. For all his stoicism, she knew he would be willing to help them in their time of need.

They would not be able to go to their homes. Even the pilot may have been identified by now. Je'Nea thought about who she knew that could hide them. She remembered there used to be a secret society known only to Empaths. She had heard Corben's father mention them, instructing her to contact them upon her arrival on Deronus.

When she had landed, they were already waiting for her and had taken her to a compound, a safehouse within the city. That had been so long ago. Perhaps she could find it again. They could hide there until she figured out something better.

Je'Nea could sense when the ship pulled closer to the planet; the tension radiating from the driver was palpable. However, Je'Nea felt something else. Corben felt it too. He sat up and pushed away from his mother, standing up in the low bowels of the ship to listen.

He looked at his mother and then they both yelled to the pilot to take off quickly. But, startled and late to respond, Selera slammed the ship to a full stop then zipped away from the surface of her docking pad. Blasters clipped the edge of her ship as she pulled out of range. Nedra stared hard at her in surprise.

"Well, that answers the question of whether we can land at my hanger or not."

"You seriously thought your place would be a good idea to land after a prison break? Really?"

"Well, I didn't exactly hear you making any suggestions, hot shot! I suppose you keep a posh place for a girl to land her ship for a quick rendezvous? Do tell!"

"No, I don't. No need to be rude. I knew we couldn't go to your place, though. You should have known the Agents would be watching and waiting for us there."

"Technically, they aren't waiting for me. So, yeah, I thought I could go home."

Nedra was begrudgingly silenced by that comment. She didn't have any better idea, either. She dropped her head in her hands, squeezing back angry tears. She had not thought this plan all the way through.

Je'Nea looked to Corben and he nodded his head. He had heard it too. They needed to move expeditiously. The rendezvous spot would not be clear for long. Je'Nea turned and addressed the pilot.

"There is a place we can dock the ship if we hurry. There are people waiting for us at the Intergalactic Space Station. Bay 7 is being held for your ship."

"What? Nonsense!. Why the hell would I go to a major transport station? It should be swarming with Agents by now."

"It was earlier, but some Empaths have taken it over and are keeping it clear for our arrival. Not exactly reading minds but making suggestions that there is a ship there that the Agents already inspected. When your ship docks, no one will notice. Except our allies."

Selera peered at Je'Nea in astonishment. How could she not know the woman and child were Empaths? Her emotions cycled from wonder, to distrust, to excitement.

"Scathingly brilliant idea! Hide in plain sight. I love it! Off we go, then."

Selera turned the ship and zipped toward the intergalactic station. She was over the anger of Nedra's miscommunication. She loved a challenge and this certainly would be one. She was now a fugitive from the law, along with her guests. This would boost her fees for travel and export from now on. A win-win, if they survive this.

Je'Nea and Corben sat close together in the cargo hold, their eyes closed and ears twitching. They seemed to be in deep concentration, as if listening to something faint. They were in communication with a very powerful Empath at the station. The message they received instructed them to remain calm. Their safe passage to the Council would be guaranteed. Je'Nea sighed softly in relief, though she did not let her guard down. She was still a mother concerned for her child. She knew the Agents would love to get their hands on Corben now that they knew about him.

The small scout ship made its way to the intergalactic docking station, found the designated bay, and docked easily. Selera, the pilot, waited, holding her breath, anticipating trouble, her hand on her weapon. There came a knock and she opened the ship portal.

Corben leaped out the door and into the waiting arms of his teacher, Inja Pyr. Beside her stood a muscular young man. He introduced himself as Cherge Den. Je'Nea nodded to him in recognition as the Empath who guided them. She took his offered hand to exit the ship. Nedra and Selera followed.

The small entourage hurried through the bay to the closest exit into the city. They walked unharassed, Inja and Je'Nea each holding Corben's small hands. He seemed familiar with the route they were taking.

They soon found themselves in a cramped alleyway leading to the back of a house. They climbed the metal stairs to the second floor of the camelback house. Waiting for them in a light airy room, sat a large-sized man, drinking tea and eating scones. Paul, the leader of the local faction of the Remnant, welcomed them and asked them to join him in the chairs set around the wrought iron table.

Selera chuckled to herself at the madness of it all and did not hesitate to help herself to the tea and scones.

Nedra was grateful the tension between them seemed to have dissipated. Je'Nea sat close to Corben, a little jealous of his affection for his teacher, Inja Pyr. Cherge Den excused himself from the room. They each accepted the cups of tea and quietly ate their scones. Paul broke the silence.

"We are delighted to have you as guests here. We are happy that you arrived safely. We are sad that you endured the discomforts and indignities caused by a brazen and insensitive government. However, that regime's time is over. The revolution has begun and we will again have unity and harmony among our citizens."

Je'Nea studied his face as he talked. Something about his speech was familiar. She could not place it though. Everyone seemed at ease, though Je'Nea felt a nagging at the back of her mind. There was something she could not quite understand. She enjoyed the offered tea and slowly consumed the scone she shared with Corben.

After introductions and refreshments, the small entourage was escorted by Cherge Den to their quarters. Je'Nea opted to take a shower first, to wash away the grime and experience of being tortured. She returned to her room refreshed. Selera and Nedra took turns in the shower as well. Je'Nea took Corben to the collective bathroom for a bath. Once every one was clean and dressed in fresh clothing, naps seemed in order. They crashed in their rooms for a much needed rest.

CHAPTER TEN

Nedra awoke first. She was unsure where she was and if the last few hours had been a dream. Body aches and sore muscles quickly confirmed the events had been real. She took in her surroundings, noting the sparse furnishings and lack of decor. She remembered.

Pale sunlight shone through the single small window. Nedra could hear birds chirping nearby. She rose from the hard bed and left the room, seeking relief from an urgent bladder. As she padded down the hall, the door to her right opened and Je'Nea peeped out. They exchanged smiles and nods as Nedra hurried to the restroom.

Je'Nea gathered toiletries and clean clothing to prepare for the day, careful to be quiet so she did not disturb the slumbering child in bed. She smiled down at Benny's sleeping baby face, his youth and innocence reminding her of little brown cherubs. His short locs framed his small head, hiding the genius within. She basked in the warmth of maternal love for a moment more, then she turned her mind to the seriousness of protecting him.

Je'Nea thought back to the penal colony to which she was immediately taken when she turned herself in to the Security Agency. The torture and experiments that were inflicted upon her would be fresh in her memory for a long time to come. She had thought she was hallucinating when Nedra opened her cell door to rescue her. Then she had panicked when she believed Corben was trapped in the bowels of the Cone Nebula prison. After a harrowing escape, they had barely survived the journey back to Deronus.

Despite their seeming safety, Je'Nea was uncertain about their present situation; it seemed somewhat precarious. She kept her senses alert and observed all she could. The layout of the house and the people practicing karate moves in the yard bothered her. She wanted news of the state of the world.

After taking her turn in the restroom, Je'Nea checked on Benny again, still sleeping. She wandered to the open room where they had met the leader, Paul. There she found him, seated at the wrought iron table, sipping tea and watching a viewer intently. Nedra sat across the table with her own viewer, her face rumpled at the images.

Nedra looked up as Je'Nea approached. "The world has turned upside down", Nedra quipped, handing the viewer to her. With a wave of her hand, Nedra rewound the article so Je'Nea could see it from the beginning.

On the screen, images showed grey-clad Peacekeepers storming neighborhoods, rounding up citizens, scattering children. The fear was palpable and Je'Nea's heart was heavy with emotion. She felt the children's terror and the adults' dread. Tears formed in her eyes and she choked on a sob. She could not continue to watch her neighbors' lives spiral into chaos. This was not what peace looked like.

Je'Nea handed the viewer back to Nedra. She wiped her eyes and tried to contain her expanding emotions. Being an Empath was difficult, but she had learned to manage her outward appearance. At least, she could appear calm until she could dissipate the swelling emotions inside her. This turn of events triggered deep feelings of empathy for herself and everyone around her.

Je'Nea felt the frustration and disappointment that Nedra experienced, knowing she would no longer be able to perform her duties as a Security Agent. Not only had she deserted her job, going AWOL, but she was a criminal now for aiding and abetting a fugitive. The list of crimes against her were staggering to even think about. She wondered how she could get herself in so much trouble? How she could get in trouble for doing the right thing? For saving Je'Nea.

Je'Nea felt something else too. Something less clear, shrouded. She sensed an insincerity, a muted... jealousy? She glanced at Paul and their eyes met briefly, before he turned back to his viewer. She was confused by the swirling emotions inside. Sometimes, she misread the feelings when they were so strong. Being used as an emotional guinea pig in the Nebula certainly did not help her now, with her nerves still raw from the torturous images they forced her to experience.

Nedra touched Je'Nea's arm and drew her attention back to the present. She looked concerned, questioning. Je'Nea smiled weakly to reassure her. She knew Nedra had sacrificed everything for her. She didn't know how she would ever be able to make this up to her. She had changed her whole life, ended her career, and turned her into a wanted criminal.

Despite her concern for Nedra, Je'Nea could not shake the feeling of ...of what? Of contempt? Je'Nea looked at Paul again. Something about him disturbed her, but she could not place what it was. She watched his movements as he pretended not to notice her. She noted the way he seemed surrounded by delicate things, the fine china, people's lives, yet he grasped the dainty teacup with a full meaty hand instead of using the handle. He consumed his scones and tea biscuits in big bites. His movements were big and he seemed to lord over everything around him. Je'Nea felt uncomfortable watching him and lowered her eyes.

As if on cue, Yacob Orin appeared in the room. He rushed to Je'Nea's side and hugged her when she stood up in surprise. She returned the hug, genuinely glad to see him. She wondered about his safety when she saw the video of the raids in her neighborhood. Association with Empaths was just as dangerous as being one, and he had aligned himself squarely with protecting those he knew about. He had been welcomed into their small circle after he had revealed that he regretted being part of the raids on Daiton.

Je'Nea pulled the chair next to her closer so Mr. Orin could sit close and they could catch up on events since they were apart. She had missed him, had taken his presence for granted, had needed his protective friendship as much as he had needed hers. She asked about the other Empaths in the community. He confirmed that they had escaped the city before the raids began.

The Remnant, as the protesters started calling themselves, were demanding equality for Empaths and exposing the government for the authoritarian suppressor it was. Airways and digital billboards were being hijacked and the truth about implants was blasted everywhere. They exposed the dangers of chipping infants and the continued existence of chronic diseases despite the claims that these had been eliminated. The truth was these people with failed chips were exiled outside the cities. They even exposed the constant surveillance of citizens by the Security Agents, not for safety reasons but to monitor behaviors. People were enraged and demanded full disclosure from the government agencies. Politicians were being expelled from leadership by emergency recalls. People called for re-elections.

Yet, fear still permeated the planet, fear of the unknown, fear of Empaths. So many lies had been told and believed for so many years, that people generally feared the powers of Empaths. They feared their thoughts could be controlled by Empaths, even though scientific studies documented that Empaths only feel what another person feels and do not have the ability to control another person's thoughts.

However, there were people who possessed the ability to project images to camouflage things. These people were powerful indeed, as they could deceive others. Some of the teachers at Benny's school possessed this special talent and they used it to protect the location of the school. This was made easier by the structure of the building itself, which was covered with reflective material so trees and grass were projected back to unsuspecting viewers. Only those people who were expected and had the exact coordinates could find the school.

Of course, there were people who possessed this talent and used it for less scrupulous means. They used their abilities for self gain and did not care who they deceived if it benefitted them. These people fueled the fears of citizens as they became aware of their presence.

Paul revealed he had this ability. Je'Nea wondered if he used it for good or evil. She was not fully convinced that he had their best interest at heart, yet. He said he used his ability to camouflage the safe house in which they were staying. She suspected the luxuries they experienced were secured by his powers as well. She wasn't sure how she thought about this.

Je'Nea contemplated Cherge Den and his place in this chain of command. He was obviously an Empath, a very talented one, who could communicate with other Empaths. He had been the presence that guided them to the docking station. Je'Nea sensed no malice at all in this man. She trusted him.

Inja Pyr, Benny's teacher, was a strong projector. She helped hide their ship when they docked and protected them on the way to the safe house. Je'Nea sensed an ability to empathize within Pyr, more like that of average humans. Yet, her commitment to the cause of the Remnant was unfailing.

This small band of people were all focused on protecting little Corben Sincera. The whole group coming from the Cone Nebula were seen by medical staff at the safehouse upon arrival. Benny's bruises and health were evaluated after the trauma of being caught, as well as the exposure to radiation.

Empathic abilities were usually marked by high levels of oxytocin in the body. Benny's labs revealed his oxytocin levels were off the charts. Paul decided he should have a security detail at all times and appointed Inja Pyr and Cherge Den to continue to watch out for his safety.

Je'Nea was thankful for all the attention being paid to her son, but she still sensed they were in danger, though she could not discern the culprit. She decided to take their security into her own hands. She prepared a pack of supplies for herself and Benny and kept them hidden in their room. When the time came, she planned to sneak away from the safe house.

CHAPTER ELEVEN

Jerika Ano located herself outside the city barriers. She tried to blend in with the people who lived independent from the technologies provided by the benevolent government. They lived by their own rules.

Jerika felt contentment, happiness, caring, concern, and love among these people. She saw them help each other and they helped her too. She was given a used tent and a few essential supplies to get her started. She was grateful and helped others when she was able.

The only discontent Jerika sensed was when grey-clad Peacekeepers appeared at the edge of the cities and invaded colonies. They called the people "the Unregistered". It was a derogatory term used because these exiled people refused to receive the cerebral implants that allowed Agents to monitor the city citizens.

The Peacekeepers came searching for children. If they found a child or teen with an implant, they captured the child and returned him or her to the cities. If they found a very young child without an implant, they took him or her to be processed and chipped. The children were fated to go to government sanctioned orphanages. Their parents were left to grieve outside the cities.

Therefore, everyone wore hooded clothes to make it harder to tell ages and children were quickly sequestered into tents to avoid detection. The hoods also protected people from the sand storms and winds that could rub your skin raw. They also coated their faces with a thin layer of oil from animal fat to prevent chafing. It gave them a slightly dirty look.

Jerika assumed the habits of her environment. She also found others with skills like hers. There were a few Empaths in the community she joined and they revealed themselves to her. They were able to be themselves and did not hide their abilities from their neighbors. Nor did their neighbors discriminate against them. Those who were able to project helped hide children from the Peacekeepers.

Jerika possessed the ability to project, but she could not sustain it for long. However, she was a powerful Empath. She felt the emotions of her neighbors strongly. It almost overwhelmed her at times. They expressed their emotions freely unlike the citizens in the city, who were used to muting their emotions, especially since there were few anxieties not already eliminated by medical and technological advancements. Nevertheless, she preferred this free expression of emotions as they were usually joyful ones.

Though this new experience enticed her, Jerika knew she had to return to the city soon. She knew there was an unavoidable necessity for change. Citizens could not continue to live in the dark, ignoring the control being exerted upon them, the invasion of privacy, the harm being done to their children by the implants, the suppression of emotions stunting their mental development. She had to answer the siren call of revolution.

Dressed in unisex clothing typical for this city's dwellers including a cloth hat to cover her shorn hair, Jerika Ano found the weakest point in the protective barrier around the city. She took a deep breath and stepped through, entering the city near the edge of a marketplace. She recognized the area and quickened her steps to seek shelter under a curved archway, away from the probing gaze of a nearby Security Agent.

Jerika noted that there were more Agents positioned around the market than normal. Security had increased because of the escapees from the penal colony in the Cone Nebula. It was assumed that some of those who escaped traveled to this planet and dispersed throughout the large cities. She was one of those escapees, and she was sure the Peacekeepers and Security Agents were actively searching for her. Commandant Oslo Ravinow would not let his prize prisoner go so easily.

Paying careful attention to the location of Security Agents and Peacekeepers, Jerika made her way through the city toward the safe house she had heard about years ago, hoping it still existed. As she journeyed, she began to sense a familiar aura. The further into the city she traveled, the stronger the feelings. She felt the potent emotions of a young child. Apprehension, fear, and confusion washed like a tidal wave over her. She recognized the signature feelings of young Corben Sincera, her former pupil. But he was supposed to be safely in the Exodus community; at least that is where he was supposed to go when his class escaped the raid on the school.

Jerika focused on the child and began to travel toward him. At the edge of the marketplace, she saw Benny and his mother. She also saw a Security Agent standing near them. The Agent began to move in their direction just as Jerika was getting closer, but she knew she would not make it to them first. She stood still and began to focus her attention on the area where the mother and child were, to project the image of a tall plant there. She hoped it would last long enough for the Agent to lose interest. Just as she was about to give out in fatigue, the Agent turned away.

Breathless with exertion, Jerika rushed toward the pair, putting her finger to her lips as warning for Benny to remain quiet. She reached and squeezed Je'Nea's shoulder in greeting. A grateful smile on her face, Je'Nea nodded to the headmistress. Jerika turned and led them around the edges of the marketplace back to the weak spot in the city barrier. She led them to the outer realm and the land of the Unregistered. Once safely resting in Jerika's tent, the adults shared the story of their journey back to Deronus. Nedra had made a huge sacrifice when she saved each of them, including Benny.

CHAPTER TWELVE

Nedra rose late from a fitful sleep. After her visit to the shared bathroom to get dressed, she stopped at Je'Nea and Benny's door. Knocking softly, she waited for a response. Getting none, she knocked louder but still received no response. Perhaps they were already in the great room with Paul. She continued to her own room and placed her things in order, making her bed.

Entering the great room with sunlight streaming in, Nedra was surprised to see only Paul, Cherge, and Inja sitting at the bistro table. They were engrossed in a lively conversation but acknowledged her entry. She joined them at the table. Interrupting their greetings, she asked where Je'Nea and Benny were. At her words, the three jumped to their feet. Paul's face turned beet red, anger narrowing his eyes.

"Go look for them, now!"

Inja and Cherge sprinted out the room and down the stairs into the street on their mission. Paul excused himself from the room, ignoring Nedra's confused questions. Nedra was left standing alone in the mist of the sun-drenched room. She shrugged in sorrow and walked back to her room.

Mind churning, Nedra allowed a great depression to overtake her. She had been used. Je"Nea had used her to avoid being discovered. She enticed Nedra and seduced her so she would help get Benny to his illegal school. She made her feel obligated to rescue her from the penal colony. Mr. Orin was in on it because he told her where they took Je'Nea. Once she and Benny were safe, they didn't need her anymore, so they left, without her.

What was Nedra supposed to do now? She went AWOL for her, for them. All she could think to do was go back to the Agency. She could give them all the information she had, about the safe house, about Paul, about all of them. That is exactly what she had to do. She had to convince her superiors that this had been a fortunate opportunity and she had taken it. Maybe she could leave out the part about the ship and Selera. She could convince them that she solicited Selera's help without telling her anything.

Nedra stopped to wonder about Selera. She had not seen her since the first night they arrived. The pilot had eaten her fill, then gone back to her room with a handful of goodies for later. Nedra stopped in her tracks and turned to knock on Selera's door. No answer. She knocked again, more persistently, but still no answer. She jiggled the handle and the door opened wide. The room was empty save a few crumbs on the nightstand.

That was it! Selera had jumped ship the first night. Nedra turned to Mr. Orin's door and bammed with her fist. She heard creaking and shuffling as the old man rose from his bed and came to the door. Surprised, Nedra grabbed his arm and demanded to know if he saw the others leave. He looked bewildered, repeating her question.

"Leave? Who left? When? Where is Je'Nea and Benny?"

"They are gone. I don't know when or where. But Je'Nea and Benny are definitely gone. So is Selera, since the first night. They all snuck off without saying a word. I'm surprised you are still here. I guess Je'Nea used us all!"

Nedra dropped her hand from Mr. Orin's arm and slumped her shoulders, shaking her head. She was even more determined than ever to return to the Agency and report them. She turned to her room gather her stuff, leaving the old man to ponder what she said.

Before Nedra could pack a single item, she heard a commotion coming from the great room. She returned to her open door to look down the hall. There stood a Peacekeeper, laser gun pointed at her head.

"Nedra Landier, you are wanted for treason, abandoning your post, and aiding a criminal. Come with me now."

Defeated and dejected, Nedra complied, raising her hands with palms out. The Peacekeeper motioned for her to move down the hall. She saw another Keeper leading Mr. Orin with a laser pistol at his head. They were guided to an airship and boarded without incident. They knew they would be killed instantly if they resisted. Kill first, provide answers later.

Peering out the window of the ship, Nedra saw that the safehouse had been raided. She saw all the other people hiding there being forced onto ships. She also saw who was not being forced. In the midst of the raid, Paul stood confidently, talking and laughing with the Commandant as if they were old friends. It dawned on her that Paul must have turned them all over to the Peacekeepers. She watched him until he turned and peered at her through the ship's window. She sat back in her seat, fighting back tears of anger and sadness.

Nedra thought of the rumors she heard about Peacekeeper raids. They were not known for their gentleness or understanding. They were strictly "by the book" special agents who followed commands with precision. They did not ask questions. They were also given license to kill if necessary. She did not dare to argue or identify herself as a Security Agent. How would she explain being in the safehouse without her uniform or consent from her superiors? Besides, she knew they had scanned her cerebral chip and already knew who she was. As if in confirmation, the Commandant boarded the ship and sat across the aisle from her.

"Security Agent Nedra Landier. We seem to have a conflict. You are pledged to 'Be present, be observant, be courteous.' Not to be a criminal yourself. You have violated your oath."

The Commandant paused for a moment. The intense burn of shame enflamed Nedra's cheeks. She could not answer. She lowered her eyes and head in shame. What could she say? He continued.

"You will be dealt with harshly for violating your oath. But your benefactor seems to think you may be useful in recapturing the criminal Empath called Je'Nea Sincera and her dangerous offspring. I, of course, think you should be punished immediately for your transgressions. However, I am not in charge. I, too, must follow instructions. You seem to have forgotten this, but will be given a chance to redeem yourself."

Commandant Ravinow rose and walked to the pilot section of the ship without another word. Nedra sat alone with her muddled thoughts. She knew where her loyalty lay. Je'Nea had used her and betrayed her, leaving her to be captured by the Peacekeepers. She was shamed in the face of her colleagues. She would never live this down, no matter how loyal she was from now on. She would always be viewed as a traitor and would, no doubt, be demoted to the worst duties. Right now, she

concentrated on how she would locate and capture
Je'Nea.

CHAPTER THIRTEEN

The grey ships landed at a military installation located in the intersection of the three large cities on Deronus. The prisoners from the safe house were escorted into adjacent cells. They could not see each other but could hear clearly and converse.

Yacob Orin called out to Nedra. He did not receive an answer. He called out a little louder, just above a whisper. Still no answer. He tried again at a normal speaking level. No answer. This disturbed him greatly. He saw her being placed in the cell once removed from him. He could only imagine what she must be feeling right now. He had served the Keepers once. They did not forget betrayal.

"Nedra. I know you are conflicted. Do not believe what they tell you. You know the truth now. You know how people are being mistreated and how your fellow citizens are being misled. Don't let them mislead you again. You must fight what they programmed you to believe. You know it is not true."

"Shut up! You know nothing of me, old man!"

Yacob shrunk at the hissed command. However, he resolved to not give up. He was grateful at least for a response finally. He tried a different tactic.

"You are an Agent first and foremost. You must follow commands. You must also discern when assistance is needed. Do you feel that anyone here is in danger? Even though you don't have your helmet, you can still sense the presence of danger. What do you feel?"

Nedra lay down on the bunkbed in the corner of the cell. She closed her eyes and tried to relax. She did not sense any immediate danger. But, after relying on her helmet for so long, she felt inadequate to fully assess the situation. She considered what she did know. The Commandant said he did what he was told to do. That meant he was not in control. Then who?

Nedra followed the recent events in her morning. She remembered seeing the Commandant talking with Paul. She recalled Paul looking directly at her while he spoke. But he was the leader of the Remnant. He was the guardian of the safehouse. Yet he was furious when he learned that Je'Nea and Benny were gone. Perhaps he influenced the Commandant to think he was harmless. But he looked comfortable with the Commandant and his smile was confident, not reassuring. At least, not reassuring to her.

Nedra thought of Je'Nea and Benny. They would have been captured if they had stayed at the safehouse. It was probably a good thing they were gone. But why did they leave? Did Je'Nea know something would happen? Did she inform the Peacekeepers that they were there? Nonsense. The Keepers would have zoned in on her and found her immediately. That is really who they want, right? They might let everyone else go if they could catch Je'Nea. Nedra's mind swirled in confusion. She was grateful Je'Nea and Benny were not at the safehouse to be captured, but she was not sure if they were safe. Still, she resented that they left her there to be captured and herded like a criminal onto the Peacekeeper ship.

Frustrated and dejected, Nedra tossed onto her side with her back to the cell door. She ignored Yacob's entreaties. She did not have to answer to him. He might be a decoy, used to feel out information from her. She would not answer anymore of his questions. She stared at the blank wall until she drifted off to sleep from shear boredom.

CHAPTER FOURTEEN

The narrow trails between tents outside the city were mazelike and confusing to Je'Nea. She followed close behind Jerika Ano as they walked quickly from her tent to the area occupied by the Council. The Unregistered, as they were called, governed themselves peacefully by way of a general council nominated by each sector. Je'Nea and Benny felt safe among the Unregistered, but they did not have time to get lost by sightseeing.

Je'Nea held Benny's hand tightly as they traversed the uneven terrain. They were careful to step over small children sitting in the pathways, where they had wandered from parents' tents, before being scooped up and returned to a surprised mother or father or sibling. These children wore dingy clothing but looked kempt and happy.

The general feeling was pleasantness, though Je'Nea could feel a tension growing. Some of the escapees from the Cone Nebula had been absorbed into the Unregistered territory. For the most part, they were not troublemakers but their mere presence made everyone vulnerable to increased interference by the Peacekeepers as they searched for them.

Many of the people who escaped from the Nebula and those who lived as Unregistered were Empaths and others with advanced mental capabilities. Je'Nea felt a kinship to those around her. As they hurried along toward the Council, she nodded to those with whom she made eye contact, a silent acknowledgement of their existence.

Arriving at the Council area, Jerika Ano led Je'Nea and Benny into the center tent. There they were greeted by an elderly man with dark brown skin and thick ropes of white hair wrapped into a cloth around his head. He sat with several other elders, male and female. They sat on the ground in a semicircle, where they could see each other's faces. Je'Nea greeted each of them with a half bow. She prompted Benny to do the same. The man motioned for them to take a seat before them.

"I am Broadus of the Elders. We welcome you."

The elderly man picked up a small metal bowl with what appeared to be oil in it. He dipped his pointer finger into the clear viscous liquid and spread it around the lip of the bowl in a slow circle. The bowl began to vibrate and a pleasant tinny hum filled the tent. When he completed the circle and stopped, the sound slowly dissipated. Broadus placed the bowl down on a square piece of brightly colored cloth and began to speak in a deep voice.

"We, the Elders, feel our world is changing. We cannot remain in the fringes of this planet any longer. It is time that we must become a part of the whole society. It is time for the whole of society to change and to include us. The time is now. We must proclaim our right to exist in this world as our true selves."

Je'Nea nodded in agreement and stated that she and little Corben will help in any way they can. She knew they could not hide anymore. Her fear for Corben took a back seat to her conviction that things had to change for his future. She remembered the uncomfortable feeling she had while in the safehouse. She knew something significant was happening but she did not know exactly what.

Je'Nea felt Nedra's distress give way to desolation. All she could hope is that she would get a chance to explain why she left without her. She knew their paths would cross again, if for no other reason than that she missed Nedra's protective presence. She knew she felt more than that for the woman, though.

As the Elders arose from their seats, everyone dispersed to their respective sections to inform their neighbors and prepare. In the morning, they would invade the cities.

CHAPTER FIFTEEN

Commandant Oslo Ravinow opened the door to Nedra's cell and entered with self-important bravado. A Peacekeeper placed a chair in the small cell and Ravinow sat facing her. He chuckled at the sight of her, dejected and alone after giving up her position as Security Agent for a jilted love. How ridiculous she must feel after being used like a tool.

"Agent Nadier. You have been accused of desertion and insurrection. But... I understand the strong pull of heart strings too well, I admit."

Nedra closed her eyes briefly, a pained look crossing her face. She opened them and looked determinedly in the face of the Commandant. She would accept her sentence with honor.

"Since you were obviously duped into betraying your government, we will be lenient. We will give you another chance to serve. You will help us find the Sincera insurrectionists and defuse this situation. You have one minute to think about it and to accept your fate."

The snarl on Ravinow's face only matched the discontent in Nedra's heart. She nodded and accepted without hesitation. She wanted this to end quickly, so she could return to the quiet predictable life she enjoyed as a Security Agent. Ravinow stood up and nodded curtly. He left as swiftly as he arrived, the Peacekeeper following him with the chair in hand. Nedra resigned herself to her fate. She would bring Je'Nea in and end this torment for good.

She lay down on her bunk, her mind swirling with plans of how she would find this woman and capture her. She was so entrenched in her own thoughts that she barely heard the voice of the old man Yacob Orin calling to her. She tried to ignore it for a few minutes, but he persisted. Finally, in disgust, she answered with a gruff "What, old man?"

Taken aback by the change in her tone and the conversation he was privy to a few minutes ago, Orin stumbled over his words. He did not imagine that Nedra would betray Je'Nea, certainly not so easily without coercion. He chose his words carefully.

"Remember who you are. Surely, you only agreed to help the Peacekeepers to find Je'Nea so you could help her, right? You will not turn her in. You cannot turn her over to them. They are savages who only want to control and use people. They would exploit her abilities. They would use Corben for their own gain, not for the good of the people. You must not help them."

"Shut up, old man. I know who I am. I am a Security Agent. That is who I am."

Nedra's growling response shut down any further discussion from Orin. He shrunk into his cell. He knew the indoctrination of Security Agents and Peacekeepers was deep seated and his protest would only convict her further. He had to plan how he would help Je'Nea. How he would play his own part in the brewing scenario.

CHAPTER SIXTEEN

Je'Nea awoke early in the darkness of the following day. She lay still. She could hear and feel the softness of her son's sleeping breath against her chest. He lay curled into the shape of her. She would protect him with her very life. She knew it would come to this soon. She lay still and enjoyed the peacefulness of being a mother in the pre-dawn hours before she would become a warrior protecting her ward.

Slowly, one by one, people began to stir in the tents around them. They were packing up camp. They were preparing for war. They would not return to these tents after today. By the end of the day, they would either be free or dead. And it would be their own choice to make, not anyone else's. Full autonomy awaited them one way or the other.

Je'Nea felt Corben move ever so slightly, his breathing pattern changing to wakefulness. She watched his cherub face scrunch up then relax as he opened his eyes and peered up at his mother. He smiled, his snaggle-toothed grin eliciting a return smile from her. He raised up and threw his arms around her neck, planting a sloppy kiss on her cheek. She would cherish this moment forever.

"We have to get ready now, Benny. Let's get you cleaned up, little man."

Je'Nea stood up, still holding Corben in her arms, feeling the full weight of this small child clinging to her. She carried him to the bathing tent and helped him prepare for the day. The pre-dawn light was just starting to increase. They would have to hurry. Je'Nea could feel the air thick with apprehension. Everyone around her was getting ready. Ready for battle.

The word had spread quickly throughout the tent dwellers outside the cities of Deronus. Leaders in each region had prepared their neighbors to strike simultaneously, entering the cities and overtaking the Security Agencies by surprise. They had pooled together a special group of Empaths and others skilled in battle to engage the Peacekeepers. If they could avoid detection and retaliation, then they would have a chance. They needed more than a chance; they needed a miracle.

Je'Nea, Corben, and their neighbors entered the fringe of the city in the early dawn. Undetected, Je'Nea and Corben headed to the nearest transport station. They took the shuttle to the Peacekeepers military base in the intersection of the three cities. There, she joined other Empaths and allies.

Together, they approached the facility as quickly as possible. Those who could cast images similar to the surroundings so the perimeter cameras appeared to be working correctly until they were close enough to disable them. A perimeter alarm went off. Their presence was known.

Je'Nea and Corben slipped through a door behind a Peacekeeper who came outside to investigate. She and her son moved from empty room to empty room searching for a familiar presence they both detected. Yacob Orin and Nedra were here.

Je'Nea was careful to move along the wall in the blind spot of cameras, indicating that Corben follow her lead. They managed to escape detection until they arrived at the underground chamber where prisoners were being held in iron cells. Her heart leaped at the sight of Nedra, though she was behind bars. She looked for keys to the old locking mechanisms and found a ring of keys hanging on the wall near the entry.

At the sight of the woman and child, Yacob Orin began to speak. However, Je'Nea shushed him immediately. He cast a wistful look toward Nedra's cell, anxious to warn Je'Nea. Before he could, Je'Nea had opened Nedra's cell door and thrown herself into the woman's arms.

Feeling the unfamiliar stiffness in Nedra's body, Je'Nea pulled back from her embrace just in time to avoid the blow aimed for her head. She stepped back, pushing Corben behind her.

"Nedra! What are you doing? Why are you trying to hurt me?"

"You are a traitor to our government! You must pay for your transgressions!"

Nedra rushed toward Je'Nea. The Empath deftly side-stepped to avoid being caught. She pushed Corben roughly, forcing him to fall against the wall and out of harm's way. Yacob Orin gathered the child up and they slipped out of the room to find safety.

Je'Nea tried to reason with Nedra as she moved around the dusty room to avoid capture. Nedra disengaged and rushed to the entry. She opened a panel in the wall and pulled out a weapon. She spun around and aimed directly at Je'Nea's ankle, firing without hesitation. Je'Nea collapsed on the floor.

Nedra pulled detainer bracelets from the compartment behind the panel. She approached Je'Nea to place them on her. As she bent down to grab the woman's wrists, a swift kick knocked her legs from under her. Nedra slammed against the dusty floor and winced in pain.

Je'Nea struggled to rise up from the floor but Nedra recovered quickly and rushed her, tackling her to the ground again. They tussled for several minutes. Finally, Nedra managed to overpower Je'Nea and held her arms behind her back until she was shackled. In triumph, Nedra stood and pushed her captive toward the entry.

"Nedra! What are you doing? What happened? I came to rescue you! I don't understand why you are doing this to me."

"Be quiet. I am a Security Agent and I am sworn to serve. You are a danger and must be detained."

"A danger to whom? Think about what you've seen and what they did to you; locked you up. Who are you serving? I am not the enemy."

"Be quiet and walk!"

Nedra pushed Je'Nea forward and led her to where she hoped Commandant Oslo Ravinow's office would be. He would be pleased that she captured this woman. He would restore Nedra to her position as Security Agent. This nightmare would soon end.

Chaos surrounded them as they stepped into the upper chamber. The facility was under attack and overrun by Unregistered people. Weapons of all sorts fired, bullets whizzed across the room and lasers beamed in return fire. Many casualties lay on the floor.

Peacekeepers scattered behind furniture and computer consoles, taking aim then hiding. To Nedra's horror, some Peacekeepers even used their fallen compatriots as shields. People slid on the blood-slick floor, still firing at each other. Blood was everywhere.

Nedra had never seen such carnage before. She heaved. Before she could regain composure, her prisoner slipped from her grasp and ran toward the Unregistered liberators. Someone fired and Je'Nea fell to her knees. The back of her garment turned black from the laser blast as she lay still in a pool of her own blood. Unconsciously, Nedra aimed and fired at her attacker. Commandant Oslo Ravinow fell face down, dead from the blast.

A scream bounced above the noise as Nedra dropped her weapon and ran to Je'Nea's side. She gathered the woman in her arms, shaking her, pleading that she respond. The limp body was surprisingly light as Nedra lifted her and carried her out of the room. The weapon fire had died down as the Unregistered victors overtook the facility.

No one detained Nedra as she carried Je'Nea out of the building. Hot tears streamed down Nedra's face. They fell on the rumpled cloth bunched and burned at Je'Nea's chest where the blast had ripped through her body, and her blood soaked into Nedra's clothing. At the sight of Yacob Orin and Corben in the sunlight, Nedra stumbled and cried out "Help!"

A doctor rushed over to her and medics took Je'Nea's body on a gurney to the makeshift clinic they had set up next to the Peacekeepers station. Nedra stared at them then crumpled into the sand as Benny screamed and tried to run to his mother's side. Yacob Orin grabbed and held the little boy tightly.

"Wait! Corben, you must wait. Let the doctors help her first."

"No, no, no!" screamed Benny. "I can't feel her! Let me go! Mommy! Mommy! Come back! Mommy!"

Mr. Orin held the child tightly, rocking him as he collapsed in his arms. He knew the worst had happened. His eyes squinted at the sight of Nedra crying in the sand, blood smeared all over her clothing. He knew without explanation. Nedra's determination to prove herself had caused Je'Nea to lose her life.

CHAPTER SEVENTEEN

The fight was over. All over the planet, the Unregistered citizens had overthrown the security agencies. The central government leaders had been captured. The Peacekeepers had been subdued.

City citizens had joined the fight with the tent dwellers and declared all people free and equal. The Empaths would be able to live in the cities freely, unmolested. Freedom rang in the air as people celebrated and cheered.

At the same time, relatives shed sad tears at the loss of loved ones in the bloody battles. This day would serve as a memorial to the lives lost. It would also be a siren to the cry for freedom.

Mr. Yacob Orin turned his back to the scene of carnage. He held Benny in his arms and rocked him. They both needed comforting. In the blink of an eye, their lives had changed forever.

With a violent thrust, Corben broke away from Yacob Orin and he sprinted as fast as his young legs could carry him toward his mother. He collapsed at her side and shook her body, pleading with her to return to him. He placed his cheek against her arm, tears streaming down his cheeks onto the blood-stained makeshift cot. He cried deep gut-wrenching sobs.

Benny's sobs quieted as he concentrated on his mother and searched to feel her presence again.. He smiled through salty tears when a hand touched his head. He raised his head and saw his mother's soft brown eyes looking back at him. He beamed a snaggle-toothed grin. He knew everything would be all right.